YA

| the absolute value of -1 |

OCT 2012

W1

|-1|

steve brezenoff

 carolrhoda LAB

MINNEAPOLIS

Carolrhoda Lab™
An imprint of Carolrhoda Books
A division of Lerner Publishing Group, Inc.
241 First Avenue North
Minneapolis, MN 55401 U.S.A.

Website address: www.lernerbooks.com

Library of Congress Cataloging-in-Publication Data

Brezenoff, Steven.
    The absolute value of -1 / by Steve Brezenoff.
        p. cm.
    Summary: Four teenagers relate their experiences as they try to cope
with problems in school and at home by smoking, drinking, using drugs, and
running track.
    ISBN: 978–0–7613–5417–8 (lib. bdg. : alk. paper)
    [1. Emotional problems—Fiction. 2. Family problems—Fiction.
3. Interpersonal relations—Fiction. 4. Brothers and sisters—Fiction. 5. High
schools—Fiction. 6. Schools—Fiction.] I. Title. II. Title: Absolute value of
negative one. III. Title: Absolute value of minus one.
PZ7.B7576Ab 2010
[Fic]—dc22   2009034274

Manufactured in the United States of America
2 – SB – 7/1/11

for my father,
whom i miss every day.
and for my son,
who i hope will know
a little of his grandfather
through me.

—s.b.

The absolute value
of the difference of two real
or complex numbers
is the distance between them.

—Wikipedia

SUZANNE

A dark wood lectern, and this doctor I've met—maybe twice?—kissed me on the cheek and called me Susan.

I looked down at my dress—black and too short; Jo bought me leggings so I wouldn't be cold, but they're patterned and fun. It was the only thing at Mom and Dad's that was appropriate, this dress from the Gap. At Mom's.

It's a few years old. I wore it to the winter dance when I was sixteen—sophomore year. I went with Greg... Something. He was high, and his hair was greasy, I remember noticing. He wanted a blow job and I slapped him.

In my hands was paper, three sheets of paper. One came from Simon. I don't remember when we found time, or made use of the time, to write these things down. I couldn't read, I realized, because of the tears in my eyes, so I looked back up and tapped the papers on the lectern.

They didn't make the sound I hoped they would, and the mike fed back.

The last forty-eight had been the longest hours of my life.

I drove my father's car. I adjusted the seat and the mirrors and it didn't matter because Dad wouldn't care he wouldn't bang his knees when he got in he wouldn't get frustrated by the little switch "L–R" to select which side-view mirror. Mom sat in the back, and Simon sat next to me in the front. He was dripping wet, and no one said anything about the leather seats.

It was very late—two or three—and the lights from cars all around and the lampposts high over the LIE blurred in the sheets of rain on the windshield so it was like driving into an impressionist palette of red and white and light yellows. The wipers couldn't even keep up. The expressway was completely unfamiliar, like I wasn't native. Construction made it a new road every time you used it.

The Van Wyck and Grand Central merges were on top of me in a blink. I slammed on the brakes and stopped in time, but the guy behind me didn't; he hit us, not hard, but we jerked forward and back into our seats. The car in front of me sped along quickly, past the merges.

"Just forget it," Simon muttered. "Go."

I swallowed and glanced into the rearview mirror at Mom. From looking at her, you would have thought she hadn't even noticed the hit. Sideways at Simon, he didn't look back at me. The guy behind would be getting out.

He'd want to know if we stopped to exchange information or something. I hit the gas before he reached my window. He couldn't see us, he shouldn't be allowed to, maybe for his sake. Maybe mine.

From the lectern, faces rushed up at me, most without features, just blank ovals of flesh. Simon and Mom had their faces pointed at the floor. I stared at Simon, willing him to look up at me, but he didn't. I scanned the crowd—"crowd" like the people at a game, or a show, or a synagogue. Here's who stood out:

Simon's girlfriend, with her black eyes and black hair and black trails of tears on her cheeks. A fist tightened around my chest as I looked at her and she looked back. Back at Simon: *Look at me! Look up!*

My roommate was in the back, standing by the double doors. She had her hand over her mouth, and I didn't care she was there. None of my friends were there, off at their college towns, not flying in so spontaneously: *You're okay, right?* She'd brought my stuff from Boston. *Go home now, Kierrey. Just go home.*

Next to the girlfriend was that third-wheel boy. Eyes closed and eyebrows up: put upon?

Lily, that's her name. I'd never met her. Was she a goth? I laughed to myself and smiled, then worried everyone had seen me smile at this memorial I was smiling my father was dead and I was smiling would you expect anything less from a girl like *her*, who ruined her brother.

Faces were everything, and twenty hours of daylight with Mom and Simon and our house, and enough rooms between us to avoid each other completely and cry on our own, or wail, or rend our clothes, but we go to the fridge or the liquor cabinet or the bathroom and the others are there and here is what I think when we make eye contact:

"Her husband is dead. She is a widow."

"His father is dead, and he made out with his sister."

"She is a pervert. She wanted her brother and her father is dead."

The real Jews cover the mirrors.

Simon still didn't look up. Nor did Mom. Abe did and he pulled off his glasses like Dad would when he worked on the crossword just like Dad.

The memorial was a Wednesday—as soon as possible, and Dad was on a gurney and then in a bag and then a pine box and then a gas oven and then he was ash in a baggy and he arrived via FedEx in a cardboard box "Just get rid of it."

I stood in the back of the hall, full of dark wooden benches, with serious dark purple cushions—gravity. Like pews, but not pews, because this was not a church, not a synagogue, just like one, for the godless or those who can't get a reservation in time.

The hall was full and I didn't see faces from the back. I saw Abe's gray head far in the front. He moved his arm around Mom's shoulders and I remembered to breathe.

I'd volunteered to speak. Simon wrote something; I would read it. Mom couldn't write, couldn't talk—could barely stand up and not cry long enough to say a single sentence to one of us.

My dress was wrong, completely. I pointed my foot and held out my leg. Tights with butterflies. "They were black and I didn't think," Jo had said. She would have gone back to the store but what does it matter? It got quiet and I looked up, because it had gotten quiet, and another doctor was on the podium. He was saying something; I didn't make it out, and I barely heard my name. But I managed to walk down the aisle.

I looked down at my legs, fluttering by. The dress hung to my knees, almost, and it swung as I walked, like I was flirting and disgusting.

"Simon . . . ," I started, thinking I'd read his first, but it caught in my throat when he looked up. I dropped my head and looked at the yellow, crinkled paper, his shaking handwriting and adorable stanzas.

I looked up at him again, coughed. I felt myself push my hair behind my ear, and it fell right back out. I wanted to claw it out.

| part one |

LILY

| chapter 1 |

Before sophomore year started, I held out hope that every other girl in my grade would have some boobs to show for their summers away. I prayed frequently that the Tits Fairy would have finally paid them all their very own visit, left them fully and well endowed, and explained very kindly in their ears to leave Lily Feinstein the fuck alone.

But September came too soon, like it always does, and even if some girls were finally filling out their sweaters, I still got all the attention. By the time I reached the end of the path from my neighborhood to the back field of the high school that first day, I'd already heard plenty. But of course no one is as sincere and positively moving as Noah.

"Hey, Lily," he called to me on our first day. He was standing, and Simon was sitting, on the steps around back, near the path from my neighborhood that hits the schoolyard. We'd started meeting there before school during freshman year, since it was a good place to smoke a couple of cigarettes before going inside. Simon is Noah's only other friend, as far as I know.

Then again, Simon and Noah were my only friends too, so I should shut up.

"I missed your tits this summer. Don't they want to come out and say hello?"

"Fuck off, Noah."

Let me stop right here. Yes, I take the lip from Noah. What am I going to do, slug him or something? I mean, I've hit him, square in the gut, a couple of times. It just eggs him on. Besides, it's his way: to be awkward and hyper and kind of retarded. He's harmless.

Simon, on the other hand, didn't even look up. His nose was in a paperback, which was bent around, so I couldn't see the title. It looked old though. The way he wears his baseball hat so low, with the brim bent so it's practically folded over on itself, I couldn't even see his eyes. Green, by the way, except right in the middle, where they are red before the black center.

"What are you reading, Simon?"

He didn't answer. Instead, he unfolded the book and held it up about an inch higher so I could squint and just barely make out *Franny and Zooey*.

"Nice to see you too."

"Ha!" Noah chirped. "Don't mind him, Lil. Mr. Fisher had an epiphany this summer and plans to get ahead on his studies."

"Exactly," Simon mumbled from behind his paperback.

Noah bounced on the top step, then stepped down to the second, then the first, and bounced some more. Three, two, one: "Yup, this is going to be a big year. A big year."

I glanced at my watch. It was 7:15, fifteen minutes before homeroom bell. That meant we had eleven minutes before I had to hit my locker.

"So," I ventured, "we have ten minutes." I shaved off one minute because I was dealing with about half a brain between the two of them.

Simon got up and slipped his book into the back pocket of his jeans. "Let's take a walk then."

Sometimes we don't just want a cigarette. Sometimes we smoke something more. Noah became even more animated as the three of us headed back up the path to my neighborhood. It's lined on both sides with a tall privacy fence, and on the other side of those fences are trees and shrubs; and beyond those: backyards; and beyond those: three bedroom homes for the familially insane. I should know.

Around the first curve, past the two maples that make a nice archway overhead, is a little inlet, where the fence on the right side was built around a public bench. I don't know exactly who put that bench there. It's bolted down into a slab of concrete, and a plaque on the back says "For My Wandering Boy—the Class of 1962." I guess some kid ran away from home, and his graduating class dedicated this bench for him. Well, I sit on it at least a few times a week, and I've never seen any wanderers hanging around, so I don't think he's coming home.

I folded up my leg and dropped onto the bench, then pushed my hair behind my ears.

Simon finally looked at my face as he sat down next to me. "Your zits are gone."

Can you feel the magic?

"I guess." I looked up at Noah, wondering when he'd sit, wishing he'd sit and give me a reason to slide closer to Simon, to make room.

Noah just bounced. He pulled off his backpack in midbounce and zipped open the small pocket on the front.

"Drum roll, please!" he said a little too loudly, and pulled out a small plastic baggie.

"Noah, man, try not to alert the whole neighborhood to our presence, okay?" Simon said. He shifted on the bench a little and pulled his hat tighter over his face.

I planted both my feet squarely on the ground, so the soles of my sneakers were perfectly flat and my heels and shins made a nice ninety-degree angle. "Five minutes," I announced.

"Shit," said Simon, and he pulled a bowl from his pocket. We passed around one pack, which Noah complained was too tight, and then started back up the path and across the athletic field to the back entrance.

"What do you have first, Simon?" I asked. He was walking right next to me; Noah was behind us. As we

fifty-yard line, I grabbed Simon by the elbow
't shake me off. Maybe it *was* going to be a

"Rohan," Simon answered. "English. He's also my independent study adviser, so I hope he doesn't suck."

"I heard he's the best English teacher to get."

"What about you?" Simon asked. But before I could answer, he added, "Noah's looking at your ass."

"I am not!" Noah insisted, and then he ran past us, jumping and hooting. Ever heard of someone who gets hyperer after smoking weed?

At the thirty, Simon cleared his throat. Seven steps later I turned to look at him, and he turned away. As we walked under the goalpost, he pulled back his arm.

"I'm going to cut through the gym." He only made eye contact for an instant, then started toward the double doors. That's more like it—good old Simon. "Later, Lil."

"Bye."

I watched him walk away a second, then turned toward the sciences wing, taking a quick look at my watch. Somehow I had lost about a minute, no doubt wasting time watching Simon walk away, so I took off like a shot—I was completely Wonder Woman. I moved that fast; my black hair flew behind me like a flag of strength. I was graceful and fleet of foot. When two senior boys suddenly burst through the back door, I smiled gracefully and winked, then slipped in behind them. They watched me go with longing in their flirty, flirty eyes.

Actually, I jogged carefully across the athletic field, holding my breasts with one arm, and my hair kept falling into my eyes, making it impossible to see, which is why when the door blasted open, I lost my balance and nearly bit it. The senior boys laughed at me. And I told them to fuck off, which only made them laugh more.

But after that, I did really smile and slip inside behind them. And I happen to think I have a very graceful smile, if nothing else.

My homeroom was exactly thirty-eight steps from the back door, including the stop at my locker to hang up my magnet-mirror and check my eyes, the redness levels of which were acceptable, I decided. I sat down in homeroom as the bell buzzed and felt the embrace and warmth of my fellow tenth graders all around me. I hadn't been early enough for the back row, which really was fine because I know what Ms. March—Math Goddess—thinks of back-rowers. I found myself pretty dead center of the room: Hal Roberts in front of me, butt crack shown for all the world to see—and occasionally toss raisins into; to my left, Lindsey Horowitz, reminding me silently that some girls have it worse than I, physically; to my right, Staci Short—I thanked myself for smoking a cigarette on the walk to school, for my own powerful stench blocked the sting of her perfume; and behind me, Elijah Rosen, who was very possibly perfect in practically every way—smiled constantly, blue eyes, shaggy hair, insanely brilliant, at least at math—and I hated him with the fiery passion of a thousand suns. When the door opened, Elijah was making himself comfy, with his foot on the back of the seat of my chair. I looked forward to spending the rest of the day with the imprint of a size ten All-Star on my ass.

Ms. March, well, marched in and swung the door closed (and locked) behind her. Her heels clicked, then clacked, in succession, until she reached her big metal desk at the front of the room. Her skirt was just north of appropriate, and her bag landed on the desk with a thud. She pulled out her attendance sheet and looked at us. "Is everyone comfortable?" she announced.

No. Elijah Rosen, I'm fairly sure, has 84 percent of his foot in my ass right now.

Of course no one actually answered. That's just not done. Besides, of course we weren't comfortable, but it would take a very brave soul to get on Ms. March's bad side sophomore year. A better plan would be to hold in all your angst until second semester senior year, after your fate is well sealed, or else take it out on someone else, like old Mr. Hoffman, who was deaf in one ear, having been too close to a jammed canon when it exploded during the Civil War. Ms. March, you see, was a very special teacher, in that her students were stuck with her not just two semesters, nor four, nor even six. No, if you act now— "now" being seventh grade, during the Research Honors qualifying exam, which I passed with flying colors—you will have the pleasure of Ms. March and her math Nazism for a full eight semesters, eighth grade right through eleventh. As a senior, you're dumped into AP Calculus. Can't wait!

Ms. March did have her good qualities, however. Two, to be precise. Quality the first: she was passionate about math, and she wanted each and every one of her RH students to become math geniuses. Some small part of me appreciated that, I suppose. Quality the second: she wore thongs.

No, I am not gay.

But I do hear the snickers of the Elijahs and Noahs of this world, so I know that the boys in my class at least had that one shining aspect of the next four years of RH math to enjoy.

So anyway, despite no one's answering Ms. March's delightful greeting, she went on: "Good, because these are your seats for the rest of the year, and you will sit in them at 7:30 on the dot each weekday morning, and you will not leave them until the end of first period at 8:42."

Suddenly she stopped. She stood there, staring down at her attendance book, unmoving. Un*breathing*. Just gazing down at that list of pathetic, awful, puny tenth graders—it seemed she'd been stopped by one name. *But which name?*

Suddenly she looked up, her mouth open, her eyebrows arched. "Clear?" That's not a name, so my internal wonderings went unanswered. But the class, this time we answered her question. I mean, not like the new recruits at boot camp who just caught on that their sergeant meant business, but it was a direct question, so to speak, so we mumbled something that could conceivably be considered the affirmative. It came out sounding like a whiny, sarcastic, "Yes, Ms. March," singsongy and all.

The first day of any class is rarely the most challenging, even RH math. Ms. March had quite a doozy of a day planned: we spent the next forty-eight minutes playing a ripping game of Last Year's Math Jeopardy! Let me clarify right away that the exclamation point at the end of that sentence is not a reflection on the joy and excitement I felt in the cockles of my heart because of this social, make-learning-fun activity. I include it only because the name of the show really is *Jeopardy!*, not *Jeopardy*.

In fact, I am never a fan of "make learning fun," nor of any in-class activity that forces me into a group of other students, especially if this grouping involves moving desks into clusters of four. And here we were, the first day of school—the first hour of school, in point of fact—and I'm schlepping furniture.

"Lily, may I speak to you, please?"

"Um," I said, turning to Ms. March. I was holding my desk with two of its legs off the floor, sort of enjoying the obnoxious screeching sound the remaining two legs made as they scraped across the tiles. "Right now?"

"It won't take long."

I dropped the desk. The two legs I'd been holding up each landed square in the center of two tiles, two tiles apart from each other, and clanked loudly. Ms. March sighed.

"What's up?"

"Lily," Ms. March opened. "I have to say, I didn't expect to see you on my roster this year."

I knew it. It was my name she had paused on for so long on that list. My heart sank a little as I thought back to ninth grade and my performance in RH2. It wasn't stellar.

"I got my grade up to a B with the final exam," I said. My voiced jumped about seven octaves. After a deep slow breath, I went on. "Mr. Green said that was enough to keep me in the program."

Ms. March stared at me, her lips curled. "Lily, I believe you should be in the program! I'm just wondering if you believe that."

"Of course I do," I said. "If I didn't, I wouldn't have enrolled in the class."

Which was true. I just hoped she wouldn't ask me to promise anything.

"Promise me you'll apply yourself this year." There it is. "It's obvious you have a gift for this material. I'd like to see you at the fair in April."

The Long Island Math Fair. Can you contain your enthusiasm?

"Okay," I said, quite intentionally avoiding the *P* word.

I suddenly noticed the room was silent. The desk screeching had ceased.

Ms. March put a hand on my shoulder. "Okay, go sit down. Let's play some Jeopardy!"

I sighed and turned back to my desk. It was now situated with three others, the only one facing the front of the room. Occupying the other three desks, per Ms. March's clear assignments, were Lindsey, Hal, and Elijah.

With a quick glance at the ceiling—and a silent *Why have you forsaken me?*—I joined my Jeopardy! team.

"You ready for this, Lily?" Elijah said at once. Then he leaned closer to me. "Do you need a smoke break first? Take the edge off a little?"

"Shut it, okay?"

So, in case you were harboring any hopes that this was going to be a girl meets boy, girl hates boy, girl kisses boy in the heat of passion, girl takes boy to the Sadie Hawkins Dance, let those hopes be shattered here and now.

By the way, a smoke break would have been very nice, thank you very much. But as that was out of the question, I reached into my bag and pulled out a spiral notebook—the blue one for math: cold. If I could have, I'd have flipped through the pages, right in front of my face, to enjoy the breeze and the smell of a clean, never-used notebook. But we can't have the entire tenth grade knowing I'm quite that huge a nutjob, so instead I opened to the first page.

It: thirty-four blue lines, pink margin, college ruled.

Me: ready to keep my head down.

| chapter 2 |

I wasn't always a cigarette-smoking bad girl. Not by any means. In seventh grade, I made a fairly conscious decision, as a matter of fact, to try on some juvie shoes over my straight laces. The best part: I know exactly why I did it and everything. That will save me so much money on therapy down the road. I figure someday, maybe during college or, hell, even after if I'm really feeling it, I'll just take the juvie shoes off, dust off my Mary Janes, and here's good Lily! Give her an A+ and a job, please.

My reasons for going bad girl are threefold:

1. Just as I was finishing my last year of elementary school, my mother went off on a cruise. She'd gone on vacations without Dad before, but only down to Florida to visit her father. For quite a few years, Mom would go down to

Florida several times per winter. Her mother died when I was very young, so her dad got lonely. This trip, though, was different. She planned on being gone a month.

"A month?" I snapped. I stomped my foot melodramatically on the kitchen floor. I was twelve, so that was completely the norm. "You'll miss my graduation!"

Yes, graduation. If you leave one school, whether you're on your way to college, grad school, the workforce, or even junior high, it counts as graduation. Not that I'm still bitter.

"Sweetie, I'm sorry," Mom replied. In my memory, she rolled her eyes and looked at her watch—tapped it twice to make sure it wasn't slow—and sighed, but I don't think she was quite that obvious in her contempt for my grievance. "Your father will video the whole thing, and you can watch it with me when I get back. You can tell me everything while we watch—like the director's analysis on a DVD."

"That's retarded." Short. To the point.

"Lily! That's an awful thing to say."

A car horn sounded out front.

"That's my taxi, sweetie pie. Will you give me a kiss good-bye?"

I didn't budge.

"A hug?" she implored.

"Aren't you even going to wait for Dad to get home from work?" In fairness, that wouldn't have meant more than a few more minutes. I wasn't asking for much.

"The taxi is here now, Lily. Not everyone is willing to wait for your father. Besides, you're old enough to stay alone for twenty minutes."

I *meant* to say good-bye.

She closed her eyes a moment and took a deep breath. Anger management is your friend. "Now. A hug, please? I love you, Lily."

Sure, drop that one on me. I looked down at the black and white tiles of the kitchen floor, installed less than a year before by a man Mom thought was too expensive and Dad thought smiled too much—especially at Mom. "Of course he smiles. You're putting his baby through college," Mom had said. You don't know real, deep pleasure until every glance at your kitchen floor reminds you of another fight between your parents, every word meant to soar miles over your head; yet if they'd known you better, they'd have realized you were being hit—square in the forehead every time.

I looked up at my mom with some hate, but mostly love, and I threw my arms around her neck. "Will you call?"

"Every day," she replied.

I cried in my room until Dad came home, then I had a tantrum about dinner. But really I was mad because he'd known already—he'd picked up takeout for two.

2. Upon reaching seventh grade, after a summer of— pardon my drama—heart-wrenching, gut-splitting,

vomit-inducing legal action, I sat down in homeroom in front of Simon Fisher. He pulled my hair.

"What?" Simon said. He squinted at me and curled his lip. A big freckle between his nose and upper lip, and slightly to the right, made it look like a bloody snarl. He didn't take his headphones off, however.

"I said, stop pulling my hair." Which he had, twice.

"I didn't touch your hair."

Mr. Kramer, our homeroom and bio teacher, looked down at his book. "Mr. Fisher," he said, looking up and smiling at us.

Simon rolled his eyes hugely, and I turned back to face forward in my chair and smiled.

"Please leave . . . Ms. . . . Feinstein alone, okay?"

"Dude, I didn't touch her!" Simon was adamant. I could have been wrong. It's possible that his desk had snagged some of my hair between itself and the back of my chair. It's *possible*.

"Good-bye, Mr. Fisher. You're off to Ms. Dean's office. Welcome to junior high school, where we do not let students call tenured science teachers 'dude.'"

As he grabbed his bag and stood up, Simon muttered under his breath something about killing me. I watched him leave. He was wearing dark, baggy jeans and a black baggy sweater with a biohazard symbol on the back. His bag was covered in patches and black and blue ink, where he'd scribbled band names.

That night I dreamed of kissing him on his bloody, snarly freckle.

3. One month into my first year in junior high, my father moved out of the house. Mom went on a date that night with a man she'd met on her cruise. He was a proctologist.

| chapter 3 |

Most days during our freshman year, Noah, Simon, and I would walk after school to the strip mall that sat on the border of my neighborhood and Noah's. Simon had to pass through Noah's anyway to get home, and I mostly enjoyed hanging out, so I went slightly out of my way.

The first day of sophomore year was no different. The three of us met at the Wandering Boy after ninth period. I was there first. Simon strolled up playing air guitar, nodding his head to the music in his ears. As he got close, he closed his eyes and smirked, very into it.

"Simon!" I got up and smacked his arm. "Take them off for once."

"All right, all right. Take it easy," he said. He pulled his headphones off and hung them around his neck, then started rubbing his shoulder like I'd really walloped him. "You work out this summer, Lil?"

"You know it," I said, and hit him in the arm. Then I started dancing around him, like a boxer.

"Hey!" he shouted. I thought he might even laugh for a second. I did earn a pretty big open-mouth grin, though, until Noah strolled up.

One of these days, I'm pulling him home before Noah can find us.

He'd seen too much.

"Don't stop bouncing on my account, Lily." He positively leered.

"You're the king of pervs, you know that, Noah?" I said. Of course, I meant it as an insult, but it didn't quite go down like that.

"You know it," Noah said with a sharp nod.

"Long may he reign," Simon added, and he pulled out his dugout—this small wooden case, totally harmless looking, but with two little compartments: one would contain weed, the other would contain a one-hitter—a fake cigarette in which to pack one hit's worth of said weed. "Pack it for us?" Simon handed Noah his apparently empty dugout.

"Leech," Noah replied, but he obliged.

"I'm good for it," Simon insisted.

I shrugged. "I'm not. Which reminds me. . . . " I'm not too proud to admit I never pay for weed or cigarettes. I may be wearing juvie shoes, but I'm not an idiot: these are shoes, not a full set of county blues.

Simon knew just what I meant. He pulled out his pack and handed me a cigarette, the reward for which was a smile from me. Noah, as usual, lit it for me.

"See? Even perv kings can be gentlemen," he explained.

"Yet Simon always gives me a cigarette," I pointed out. "Ha! That crown is a sham! Your gesture is weak, your majesty." I curtsied—I guess I was just in a giddy mood.

"I smoke menthols!" Noah said. He said that frequently, actually. "If you want a menthol, please, help yourself."

One day I'll call his bluff and smoke those disgusting things for a month just to shut him up about it.

After a few packs and passes of Simon's bat, we were all feeling pretty slow, so the walk to the Gap took a nice long time. It was warm, and my sweater was jammed into my bag. I held on to Simon's arm as Noah led the way, talking our ears off. I know I wasn't listening, fully enveloped in Simonness.

Simon wasn't listening, either, at least not to Noah.

"What are you listening to?" I asked. He'd not so slyly put his left earbud in as I grasped his right elbow.

Rather than answer, he simply said, "Here," and slipped the right bud into my left ear.

It was what I'd come to expect from Simon's headphones over the last couple of years: heavy but without much flash. It just boomed along, bass heavy and choppy—Simon's favorite music always reminded me more of a single walking figure, moving slowly, but never stopping, rather than an army of undead warriors on stampeding horseback, which is what I'd always thought of metal before.

But I'm not a music critic. What I am is a math goddess in training.

"Ooh, seven!" I said suddenly. What I meant, to clarify, was the song's 7/4 time signature. That means each measure of music contains seven beats, and each beat is a quarter note. Not that music like this is ever really written out, so the "4" part is pretty arbitrary.

The only things I enjoyed about my year of playing flute in the school band were time signatures and the circle of fifths, which is the magical place where math and music are one, perfectly represented on a wheel of majors and minors and how they relate to each other. I nearly stuck with the flute just for the math. Nearly.

Simon turned to me, shocked. "You can tell that's in seven?"

"Sure. I can count, can't I?" I said with a shrug. But my heart was in my throat.

"It's pretty sick, isn't it?" Simon said, and that was the end of it. Fifty-seven steps later, in time with the music, we reached the Gap. Noah was already stuffing his cigarettes back into his pocket, having lit his menthol.

"You guy's wanna keep this party moving at my house?" Noah said. He wasn't watching us walk up, though. He was peering into the big front windows of the Gap.

"What are you doing?" Simon asked him. He pulled his arm away from me to take out his own cigarettes, and he gave me one before I asked. "You look like a crazy person."

I laughed. What can I say. He did. He looked like an escaped nut, pacing back and forth in front of a clothing store, smoking his cigarette intensely and peeking in the windows. If anyone shopped at that Gap, they'd have been weirded right out.

"Nothing." He stopped pacing and dropped his cigarette and stepped it out. "What do you say? My house? Bong hits? Biohazard? Xbox?"

"What, did your parents move out finally?" I said with a smile.

"I wish," Noah replied. I don't know if he missed the jab that was "finally" or if he just didn't get the implied "couldn't stand living with you anymore."

"Dad's out in California for a couple of days, something about his practice—I don't know," Noah went on. "And when it comes to Mom, whatever. She'll be out in the solarium doing whatever the hell she does out there."

"Man, she probably gets high out there all day," Simon said as he sat on the curb. Noah laughed. "I bet she grows your shit too. All this talk about a connection in California and a new crop from Alaska or Canada or wherever the fuck—your Mom is your supplier."

Noah was hysterical laughing at that one.

I shrugged. "It would explain a lot, actually," I pointed out, and I sat down beside Simon. "That big house, all the paintings and sculptures and shit, and the fixing up your family did before they moved in . . ."

I turned to Simon. "Do you remember that house before Noah's dad got his hands on it?" I asked through my chuckles, but Noah was in my face in a heartbeat.

"What about the paintings and art?" he asked me, and I wiped his spittle from my cheek. "What is that supposed to mean?"

"Wow, chill, Noah," Simon said. I mean, he didn't exactly jump up and throw him to the parking lot or anything, but it was as close as I could hope for to coming to my rescue.

"It was a joke, Noah," I said with an exaggerated shrug. "You know, in movies people who deal drugs are always buying expensive things with the cash, to cover their tracks. It's called money laundering or something. It was just a joke."

"Well it wasn't funny, okay?" Noah said. He pulled out another cigarette and lit it. "I'm going home. If you guys wanna sit here all fucking night, go right ahead."

With that gem, he walked off.

"What was that all about?" I said, resting my head on Simon's shoulder. I felt him shrug under my temple.

"He probably did his whole month's Ritalin on the walk over here. Who knows."

He got up, and I looked up at him. "Going home?" I asked.

"I guess," he said. "Dinner at five, you know. Same old thing."

"Right," I said, getting up. "Guess I'll go home and do some homework."

Simon shook his head. "First night of school, Lil. Homework, really?"

I shrugged. "That's RH math, I guess."

"There is no test I was happier to fail than that," he said back, then put his earbuds in. "See ya tomorrow, Feinstein."

"Bye." As I watched him walk across the parking lot toward his neighborhood, the same way Noah had walked a few minutes before, I thought about firsts. After all, Simon was my first crush and my first friend in junior high; he was with me for my first mile around the track, his first cigarette, my first concert, and our first bong hits; this was the first day of our first double-digit grade. Suddenly I felt afraid—I don't know exactly of what. So I jumped up and called out, "Hey, Simon! Wait!"

He turned to look at me and pulled off his headphones.

I shaded my eyes from the sun, still pretty high behind him. He stood there, waiting for me to say something, to offer any kind of explanation for my outburst.

I looked back at him, and said, "Are you ready for this? Another year?"

He waved me off. "Please," he shouted to me. "Piece of cake. Don't be such a drama queen." Simon put his earbuds back in and walked on.

I sat back down on the curb, folded my arms over my knees, and rested my head. "Definitely," I said. "Piece of cake."

| chapter 4 |

I didn't immediately follow Simon down the path to delinquency. I didn't even really mean to follow him at all. My interests and his, especially back in seventh grade, did not intersect in any way, shape, or form. If an outside observer had been watching our behavior—the trends of our interactions that year—he or she might have thought Simon was in fact following me. I mean, who ever heard of a sulking, metalhead boy joining the track team?

But he did. So I did.

But that's not really why I joined, at least not in my own mind to begin with. I had myriad reasons to join.

Here's something you should know about me: I have hypothetical arguments on a pretty frequent basis. Every decision I make—on topics from an answer to a complicated math problem, to what to have for lunch, to taking a certain route from one class to the next—requires a thoroughly prepared defense. One such hypothetical argument from high school might go like this:

Noah: "Why are you having a veggie burger for lunch?"

Me: "I've stopped eating meat."

Noah: "Of course you did, because Orlando Bloom did."

Me: "That's not why at all. I became a vegetarian because animals are mistreated by major meat-producing corporate farms. They're treated as a product or a commodity, instead of like another living thing that is giving up its life so that we can have a couple of minutes of visceral pleasure."

I work through these hypothetical arguments on my walk to school, or in the shower, usually before I've fully committed to the decision in question. My opponent is always the person who will be most likely to point out a possible ulterior motive. Once the hypothetical argument has been processed, I tend to feel better about the decision, and a little angry.

The truth, of course, is that in that hypothetical argument, I'm always talking (or shouting) out of my butt, because I don't believe a word of what I'm saying. The truth is, I took the math and science wing from social studies to the gym not because I had to stop by my locker, but because I like how my feet fit into the tiles in that section of the school. The truth is, I had a veggie burger for lunch because, yes, Orlando Bloom is a vegetarian. Or possibly a vegan. I should look into that.

But back to seventh grade. My point is, yes, I wanted to stay in shape, or get in better shape, or have an athletic aspect to my college applications—all that is true. But none of that is why I joined track. I joined because Simon did.

It's not like I was stalking him or something, either. We were already friends; sitting in front of him every single day for an hour, especially since I had so successfully gotten under his skin on day one, will do that. But we definitely weren't spending a lot of time together beyond that. We flirted heavily—or anyway I did; I don't think Simon was or is capable of civilized flirting—during class, but that's all. So when I found out (through honorable means, I promise) that he was joining the track team, the little worm of doing something idiotic bored into my ear and wiggled around until I found myself counting the floor tiles from my locker to the track coach's office. The pen was in my hand when my hypothetical argument began, this time with the entire goddamn seventh grade.

But I won, as always, and scribbled my name on the sign-up sheet.

Simon seemed happy to see me at the first day of track practice. Don't be surprised I made the team, by the way. I should explain quickly that the junior high school track team is not popular. No one cares about track, which includes most of the people actually *on* track. Of the whole team, about five of us gave half a shit, and only two or three gave an entire shit, about performing to their best abilities. For this reason, and because there was no danger of overenrollment, the track team does not have tryouts.

Instead, it's more like a drama club meeting: There are auditions. A few people are selected to play the major roles, a few are selected for the minor roles, loads are thrown into the chorus, and then everyone else ends up doing lighting or pushing sets around. Everyone who shows up, though, will play some role, from Girl with the Final Aria to Girl Who Turns the Pages for the Piano Player. On track, that means a few of us are hotshots and place in meets, and the rest of us are pretty much jogging around in ugly uniforms.

Simon was sitting in the track infield. He was head to toe in blue sweats, like the rest of us—completely shapeless, baggy, and blue. For once, though, he had no baseball hat on, and his short red hair looked like I always imagined Huck Finn's would: like a badly hewn field of orange hay.

I sat down next to him on the grass. "Hi."

"Well, well," Simon said, molto snotty. "If it isn't little Miss Feinstein."

I stuck out my tongue appropriately and watched the coach flip through his clipboard.

"You're joining the track team?" Simon said after I'd ignored him a few minutes. Really I hadn't ignored him;

I'd just had no idea what to say to him. As usual. I'd covered this fact by not looking at him in as smug a manner as I could.

"Um, did you figure that out yourself?" I replied, snarling at him. My hair fell over my face as I turned to him, and I pushed it behind my ear.

He just closed his eyes and shrugged. Then the coach, Mr. Freeman, called us to attention. Freeman, by the way, also coached the high school team. Apparently he was the only member of the faculty, systemwide, willing to coach track.

"Okay, people," he said, "welcome to winter track. You all made the team."

Like I was saying.

"If you don't do anything incredibly stupid, you'll probably be on the team—if you can stick it out—until the end of the season," Freeman went on, rarely looking up from his clipboard. "Now let's get some event assignments done, and this first practice won't be a total waste of our time."

Freeman flipped through the pages on his clipboard. "First: who's interested in the dash?"

Two eighth-grade boys raised their hands.

"That's it?" Freeman said, looking us over. "Hundred-yard dash, that is."

At that, three seventh-graders raised their hands quickly, as if they might miss it or something if they didn't hurry. Freeman rolled his eyes and Simon chuckled.

"Morons," he said at me sideways.

"Okay, I think we can squeeze in three neophytes on our dash team," Freeman said. "Names?"

The new kids called out their names, and Freeman scribbled them down. Then he moved on to the 200. I was surprised to see Simon's hand shoot up. Had I been more prepared—such as, knowing that runners ran races of different lengths and had specialties, for example; in other words, knowing anything about track—I might have put my hand up too. But, as it was, it seemed too obvious, to see Simon and copy him. I figured being on the team was probably enough.

With Simon on the 200 team was just one other person, an eighth-grader who seemed pretty serious about running. He was a very in-shape-looking (one of the few people who was, first of all, not in sweats but in the team shorts and tanktop, and second, already stretching and running in place) black guy whose name I didn't know. Coach Freeman obviously knew him, though, because he wrote down his name before even looking up. Then he took Simon's.

The black guy also raised his hand for the 400, which looked to be the most popular race. Simon did too. I almost raised my hand for that one, thinking I could just slip through unnoticed, but I waited too long and then felt stupid. So I decided to raise my hand for the next one, whatever it was.

"Mile." And up shot my arm. I must have visibly cringed. Must have.

One mile. Four laps around the track. I'd never even run *one*.

"Let's stretch out a little before we do any running, okay?" Freeman said after dropping his clipboard onto the grass. "This will be our stretching routine for the season, so learn 'em now."

He showed us butterfly stretches, where you sit down with your feet together, and hurdler stretches, which were especially unpleasant, and one where you need a partner. Simon was not mine. We'd already broken off into groups (Simon said, "You're a miler? Okay," and walked off), and I was stuck with Melanie Siegel. She leaned on my shoulder and pushed onto her rear foot. This was to stretch the . . . leg muscles?

"I'm glad there's another girl doing the mile," Melanie said.

I smiled at her.

I'd known Melanie Siegel most of my life. She was adorable and smiled all the time and I wanted to punch her face. I might be projecting a little from my tenth-grade self to my seventh-grade self, but not much.

"I don't know how good I am," I said, holding her ankle so her legs formed almost a 180-degree angle for some insane stretch I didn't plan to attempt. "You look like you already know what you're doing out here."

Translation from wussy seventh grader to bitchy tenth grader: I will not be running with you. Ever. Because you sicken me.

"I'll help you out any way I can," Melanie replied, smiling (retch). Then she helped me stretch my glutes or quads or whatever the fuck.

There were five of us on the mile squad: me and Melanie; a seventh-grade boy name Robin (ouch) Goldberg; and two eighth graders, Jake and Hank. Robin was something of a school pariah: his name and meager stature made him the go-to target of ridicule and random beatings. He was a pretty good miler, though, it turned out—certainly the best on the team.

Freeman blew his whistle. "Let's do some warm-ups. One mile, everyone, even short-distance, please. And stay with your event. Let's have the milers start out first."

Melanie jogged right from the infield, onto the track, and was off. Robin was right next to her in an instant. As for me, Jake, and Hank, we sort of collectively screwed up our faces to say, *Seriously? A mile? On the first day?* Then, with a sigh and heavy hearts, we headed after them.

It didn't take long before Freeman's rule about sticking with your event had been not just broken but shattered in teeny tiny pieces. Simon caught up to me and the miler boys in about fifteen seconds.

"You three are pretty pathetic," he said as he passed.

"Screw you, Simon," I replied. Jake and Hank didn't seem to give a rat's ass. They ignored him and kept on chatting with each other. Freeman frequently told them to shut up and run.

About Jake and Hank: They were practically identical, it seemed. Same height, same hair color, same hairstyle. I couldn't for the life of me figure out why they were on the team. But they did kind of change my life.

Oh, and if you're wondering: two sports bras.

| chapter 5 |

A particle is moving along the x axis such that
its position at any time *(t)* is given as *s(t)=2sin(π)*.
What are the amplitude, frequency,
and period of this motion?

Within the first six weeks of sophomore year, I had learned four things worth noting:

1. Positive and negative numbers have the wonderful quality of being able to shed their signs to take on their "absolute value." That means a number as grandiose and huge as 58 million has the same absolute value as a *debt* of 58 million. I should be so lucky.

2. Chewing gum, when affixed to the bottom of Elijah's size-ten sneakers, has no trouble dislodging itself to better attach to my butt. Getting it off my butt, though, is much trickier.

3. Mr. Rohan walks to his car through the side door, at least on Thursdays. I know this because it was a Thursday in October that he caught me, Simon, and Noah smoking. He was especially mad at me and Simon, I guess 'cause he knows we're smarter than that. Noah, not so much.

4. Simon and Noah are obsessed with the new girl working at the Gap. When they discovered this about each other, I thought they were about to fight like hyenas over a dead gazelle. Instead, Simon won a little staring contest and they changed the subject.

Unfortunately, that soured everyone's mood, and Simon went off home, leaving me sitting on the curb at the strip mall, with Noah yabbering at me, bouncing up and down—up the curb, off the curb, around the No Parking sign, back on the curb, off the curb.

"Your parents are divorced, right?" he asked. I was going to add "out of the blue," but there might have been a good segue. I just wasn't paying close attention. But that question pulled me back.

"Yup," I said. "Their three-year divorce anniversary is right about now, actually. Why?" Not to be terse, but I was pretty much over it. The only real difference between pre-divorce life and post-divorce life for me was that my parents only fought on the phone, and rarely.

Noah kept moving around me. Simon was long out of sight.

"No reason," Noah said. "Did your dad have an affair or anything like that?"

I shrugged. "I don't think so. They just always sort of, I don't know—hated each other, I think."

"Wow, really?" he said. He took out a cigarette and lit it.

I cleared my throat audibly.

He stopped pacing and said, "They're menthol."

"That's fine." So he gave me one, and it was gross but worth it.

"Anyway, that sucks," Noah went on. "Your whole life they hated each other?"

I thought about it a minute. "I guess I don't remember my whole life. But I do remember a lot of fights and shit." I took a drag from my cigarette and tried to get used to the toothpaste-ness of it. It was futile. "Why are you asking me about my parents?"

Noah shrugged. "My parents fight a lot too," he said, and that was that.

So I went home. I said good-bye to Noah and walked back across 25A. As soon as I was out of Noah's sight, I dropped the menthol too. I couldn't let him know I'd wasted a cigarette of his. He'd never forgive me.

Mom had beaten me home. Typically, I should be getting home first like a good little latch-key kid, but I'd dawdled. Not like she noticed.

"Lily!" she called from upstairs. "Is that you?"

"No, Mom!" I called back, kicking off my sneakers. "It's the Spanish Inquisition!"

There was a pause. "What?" she called down.

"Ugh, never mind," I muttered nowhere near loud enough, then wandered into the kitchen and grabbed a can of soda from the fridge. I stood next to the counter, drinking it. Then I looked down at my feet.

The kitchen tiles, in addition to being black and white and a reminder of a dysfunctional marriage and very possibly a sexual relationship between my mother and the contractor, are exactly six and one quarter inches by six and one quarter inches. Perfect squares. Their diagonal, therefore, is 8.84 inches. That is also the length of my feet. When I stand with my heels together and with my feet at a ninety-degree angle to each other, they perfectly connect the corners of a tile each—one in a black tile, one in a white.

I'm slightly pigeon-toed. You probably wouldn't notice it if you saw me, but I am pretty aware of it most of the time. You should see my shoes. The soles are so unevenly worn, it's embarrassing. So when I stand in the kitchen, fully duck footed and connecting the corners of two tiles, I consider it compensation.

Mom walked in as I was guzzling away.

"Hi, sweetie," she said, and she put an arm around me. She had just gotten out of the shower; her hair was in a towel, and she was wrapped in a huge terrycloth robe. "Lily, you smell awful."

"Oh hey, thanks, Mom," I said. I jiggled the can to hear if any drops were left. I coaxed out a desperate sip that was probably all backwash, then put the can on the counter. "That's really awesome of you to say."

She just shrugged and picked up the pile of mail. Flipping through it, she added, "Well, you do. I really wish you wouldn't smoke. It's so disgusting. What boy is going to want to date a girl with smelly hair, and smelly clothes—"

"All right, Mom!" I snapped at her. She looked positively aghast that I'd interrupted her advice. "I get the picture!"

"I wasn't finished, and put that can in the recycling bin." I groaned and sighed and just about threw a fit, but I picked up the can and rinsed it out and dropped it into the plastic bin under the counter.

After I'd obeyed, Mom said, "And bad breath."

I rolled my eyes as I left the kitchen.

"You know it's true!" she called after me. "I'm just looking out for you, Lily-pie!"

I was halfway up the steps when the proctologist came out of my mom's bedroom, fresh from the shower himself and in one of his awful tracksuits.

"Oh, hi, Lily," he said.

I rolled my eyes at him and went into my room.

To answer your questions, no, they did not get married. He didn't even move in or anything like that. He's divorced too, and I don't suppose either of them is terribly interested in committing in any serious way. But after three years, I'd gotten used to seeing him around on occasion. And your other question: yes, they had just had afternoon sex in my childhood home, knowing full well I'd be walking in at any moment.

Thank God above I'd stuck around an extra few minutes talking to Noah, or I swear, I might have heard them climax.

| chapter 6 |

On junior high track, Jake and Hank were the best milers, by far—at least, to me. Pretty early on during my first season on the team, it became obvious why they were on the track team: when it came to the team members who didn't give any portion of a shit, Freeman was completely blind. Every day, after stretching, Freeman sent us milers up into the Hills, which is my neighborhood, for our own special run. We didn't even have to warm up with the short-distance gang. There was this very circuitous route, up hills and down hills and around huge loping curves . . . It was boring enough to put you into a coma as you ran it. Or so I've heard.

Melanie and Robin lived for it. The fact that the two of them—opposite in nearly every way: her beautiful, charming, well loved; him scrawny, acne-ridden, outcast—became friends by running this route every single day together I suppose makes it a fairly magical mystery tour. But for normal people, it was hell. Or it would have been, if not for one saving grace—the one that Jake, Hank, and I (and eventually Simon) began to take advantage of.

Once we long-distancers were on our way, Freeman's attention was focused on the 400s, the 200s, and the 100s. As long as we waved to him after our run on the way to the locker room, he would wave back and all would be hunky-dory. In other words, Jake, Hank, and I (and eventually Simon) never ran the whole route. Not once.

"Lily, Lily, Lily," Jake said as he put an arm around my shoulders. We'd just started our first long-route run of the season—my first ever. This was probably the second week of track practice; before this, we'd stuck to the track itself. Melanie and Robin were already up the first climb, and I guess I was pretty obviously betraying my dread. "I don't know about you, but Hank and I are not running all that distance."

"We might pull something," Hank explained. He shook his head. "Nothin' doin'."

With one arm still around me, Jake led us down a different side street, very nicely downhill and into the other side of the school's campus, past the tennis court and fully out of view of the track.

Before us was the district-run nursery school. It was, if my understanding was correct, essentially for working and single mothers who had to deposit their children someplace but couldn't afford day care or a nanny. Behind it was a swing set. Jake hooted and released me, then threw himself into a swing.

Hank laughed and took the swing beside him.

"Are you guys serious?" I said, looking around, half expecting Freeman to throw a clipboard at my head at any moment. "The coach will kill us."

Jake waved me off. "Oh please. That man is entirely without a clue."

Hank nodded sagely. "Indeed." He reached into his sweatshirt pocket and pulled out a pack of cigarettes.

"Oh come *on*," I said as he lit one. "You have *got* to be kidding me."

That really had them rolling all four eyes as far back in their heads as they would go.

"What?" I said in reply to their obvious disdain. "I joined track to get in shape, not to get into worse shape and kill myself."

"Ha," Hank said. "If you wanted to kill yourself, I'd just say go run the hurdles."

Jake got up from his swing as Hank handed him a cigarette. He walked over to me and lit it. "Besides, Lil— can I call you Lil?—you joined this team for one reason and one reason only."

Yes. My hypothetical argument was about to come true, and I knew I'd lost it before it had started.

"You're in love with Simon," Jake and Hank finished in unison.

I think I betrayed the truth with a smile, which had them both in stitches. When they'd recovered, I hit Jake, and Hank handed me a cigarette.

"Oh, no. I don't—" But I took it, and I smoked it—or tried to. Those two boys practically had to carry me back to the locker room, though, once I finally inhaled any of it. I got pretty seriously light-headed. Of course, that just made the whole charade look more convincing to Freeman as the three of us walked by and waved. He was probably proud of me for giving it my all.

As my guides deposited me outside the girls' locker room, Jake whispered in my ear, "Simon is going to *love* you."

I watched the two of them—hysterical—make their way into the boys' locker room, but I couldn't quite bring myself to enter the girls'.

While I was standing there, the short-distance crew came ambling in, along with Melanie and Robin. My stomach tightened as I realized it would have appeared to anyone that we beat them, two of the best runners on the team.

Robin headed into the boys' locker room, and Melanie walked over to me. She twisted her mouth into this *So disappointed, but not surprised* look. "You're friends with Hank and Jake, huh?"

I shrugged. "I guess."

"That's too bad," Melanie said.

Then she walked past me and into the locker room. Well, if you hate them, I thought, I must be doing something right.

I crossed my arms and thought about going home without changing.

| chapter 7 |

Ms. March collected our first paper in November.

"A paper," you say, "in math?"

Why, yes! That, my dearies, is the real thrill of Research Honors Math, 1 through 4: the research itself. Why let the history fans have all the fun?

On a Thursday in November, Ms. March held me after class to talk to me about the paper. She sat at her desk and I stood across it from her. In her hand was my paper, but I couldn't see the grade. She opened with, "Do you play an instrument, Lily?" My paper had been called "Circular Functions and Circle of Fifths: Applications of Trigonometry in Music."

"I did for about a second. Flute," I replied.

"Well, this is really great," Ms. March said, looking up at me and smiling. "It really is. Honestly, Lily—it's college-level stuff. I'm so happy."

I'd spent a lot of time on it, so I was pretty pleased. Mainly, though, I was happy to have proved myself as a math whiz again. I wasn't leaving this program; my whole future—the one where I finally put my Mary Janes back on—depended on it.

"Thanks," I said.

She kept smiling up at me, shaking her head. "You do know I'm thinking Math Fair with this, right?"

"Oh come on," I said. "It's not a new topic. I mean, everyone talks about the math of music. It's like a thing."

"It's new from someone in tenth grade, and put so beautifully." Ms. March stood up and handed me the paper. Then she snapped her briefcase shut. "You know the whole point of RH is to help students see the aesthetic beauty in mathematics, Lily, and you've done that on your own."

She ushered me out, locked the door behind us, and walked off. I finally looked down at the paper in my hand. I wasn't surprised to see the A, but it still felt great.

Why, then, did I skip Ms. March's class the very next day? I guess I figured I'd earned it. She had given me an A, told me I was the best student she'd ever had in her life, and that I was ready for graduate study. One missed class wouldn't hurt, especially a Friday.

Wait.

I'm doing it again. The hypothetical argument creation matrix was in full effect, and that was my half of the rationalization hypothetical argument.

Some truth: I skipped because when homeroom was scheduled to start, I was leaning against my favorite tree behind the high school, with the head of my favorite boy in my lap, and my fingers in his hair. Plus I had a very nice buzz on.

None of us moved much or said anything for probably an hour. We were pretty stoned. When the fog cleared a little, but not enough so I could think really straight, I looked up at Noah.

"What happened to your eye?" I asked him. He had a really wicked black eye. If he'd gotten into a fight at school, I definitely would have known about it.

"My dad popped me good last night," Noah replied. He got to his feet pretty quickly and started bouncing a little.

"That's 'cause his dad is a class-A fuckwad," Simon said. I had thought maybe he had fallen asleep. His eyes were closed and he hadn't moved in forever.

"Whatever, I don't care," Noah said. He pulled his bowl out of his pocket and packed it. Then he changed the subject. "There's a party at Kyle Aaronson's tomorrow night. Goody told me about it."

He passed the bowl to me and I took it, but I didn't hit it anymore. I was ready to come down, so I just passed it to Simon. "Do you wanna go?" I asked, and though I'd been talking to both boys, I was really asking Simon.

Noah answered in the affirmative, and Simon ignored the question. Instead, he asked for the time.

I checked my watch. "Second period starts in ten minutes," I said. Simon leaned forward and sat up, leaving my fingers with no hair to be in. They suddenly felt cold.

"Okay, I'm going in," Simon said, slowly getting to his feet.

Simon and I had second period together—social studies with Mr. Hillenbrand. I got up too, and Simon turned to look at me. "You coming, Lil?"

"I guess, may as well," I replied coolly. And we walked together across the traffic circle and into the school. Simon felt off, though. Not just high—sad. Normally I would have taken his arm, but I didn't. Still, it was nice to just be walking with him, talking to him.

It was during that class that Simon got called to the principal's office. He wasn't in school the rest of the day, and believe me—I looked for him. I wanted to bring him to that party so bad. I was sure that me and Simon plus some beers and a lot of people we don't like very much would end in a very good night kiss. But when Saturday night rolled around, I hadn't seen him or spoken to him since he'd looked at me with a question in his eyes and I'd shrugged back before he'd headed to Gilliard's office.

Yeah, I tried calling him on Saturday, but I got his family's answering machine or something. I'd only ever called his house like once before in my life, and I was probably around thirteen at the time. Looking for French homework, probably—something ridiculous like that. So when his dad's voice came through the phone, calmly reading back the phone number I'd just dialed, I hung up.

Noah, of course, called me.

"So are we going to this party?" Noah asked. "'Cause I'm definitely going. I have some shit to sell."

I clucked my tongue. "Have you heard from Simon at all?" It was already almost ten thirty.

"Naw, that guy's a slacker. He's not going to any house party, believe me."

I didn't respond right away. My hypothetical argument creation matrix instead kicked into gear, and I—in a matter of seconds—decided Noah didn't know Simon like I did, and that this Saturday night would be the one I'd imagined. I had no doubt at all for just an instant—long enough to agree to go with Noah to this party.

So I did. It didn't take me long to get ready; the faster I moved, getting into my favorite baggy jeans and that Kittie T-shirt over a white thermal, the less I thought about my decision to go out. A tip from the hypothetical argument creation matrix: once you've won, move fast; this is very sensitive, very precarious material. You have to handle it like C-4 on *Alias* or something.

Noah was at my house in no time at all, and I called out to my mom, "I'm going out. I won't be late."

I don't think she heard me. To be honest, I don't think she was sure I'd even been home at all. Come to think of it, I'm not actually sure *she* was home.

Kyle Aaronson's house is in my neighborhood. He's a junior, so it's not like he's a friend of mine or something. He's also not at all my type of person. He'd never stoop low enough to join track, or concern himself at all with the aesthetic beauty of mathematics. Nope. He, you see, was popular. He had a tremendous amount of teeth in his smile, which he showed often.

Noah talked a lot on the way to the party, but aside from that, he really wasn't acting like his normal self. He was definitely nervous, which is pretty normal, I suppose; but he also had this cocky thing going—forced cocky.

"I'm meeting like fifteen people at this party," he said as we headed up Wren Court. Kyle's house was up at the top of this cul de sac, on a weird little circle. The party was already going on, that was obvious. Every inch of curb in the circle had a car parked on it—mostly SUVs. The juniors and seniors at our high school are notorious environmental catastrophes, for real.

"I have more weed on me right now than I've ever carried before, I think," Noah went on.

I rolled my eyes. "That's great. When the cops show up to break up this party, I don't know you."

They did. Show up, that is. But I don't want to leave you in suspense, thinking Noah's ending up in jail or something. No one is getting arrested or shot or anything in this story. The only wounds in here will be emotional, I promise.

We went straight around to the back of the house. Most house parties around here take place out back, at full volume, with kegs. I don't know why it always takes so long for neighbors to call the police. I mean, it's always pretty obvious where the underage drinking is going on. Plus, hey, free pot dealer to bust, no extra charge.

Anyway, the keg, on the back deck, was being well manned by one of Kyle's football or baseball or something cronies. He had a big neck and, as we walked up, farted loudly.

"Whoops, didn't know there was ladies present," he said. Then he turned to Noah. "Apologies, madame." His buddies got hysterical all over themselves. Noah tried to force a laugh. I just glared.

"Cups are five bucks," the thick-neck said as his smile turned into something like the face a silverback gorilla makes from behind the glass at the monkey house. Noah paid for mine, too.

"That guy's an asshole," Noah said as we walked away, sipping our foam.

"Everyone here is an asshole," I said. I looked around, craning my neck, hoping to spot Simon. Of course, my hypothetical argument creation matrix had by this time shut down for the evening. Here, in the cruel dark of night, surrounded by people I didn't like, or know, or like to know, it hit me that Simon would never—EVER—come here, especially with someone other than me and Noah. And we were already there.

"Anyway," I went on. I noticed Noah was looking around a lot too. "They were making fun of me as much as you. He meant I'm not a lady."

"Whatever," Noah said. He touched my arm a second. "Look, I'm going to talk to Hilly a second. He's right over there. I'll be right back."

And he left me, standing there, near the back shrubs of goddamn Chez Aaronson, holding my beer. Alone.

Three senior girls who looked pretty much like I'd like to stood in a small group nearby. They were smoking, and they didn't seem like the kind that would sneer at me.

"Um, can I bum a cigarette off you, please?" I said, leaning a little way into the trio.

They did glance at each other, conspiratorially. But girls do that—so I've heard. And the tallest one, who had a serious retro hairstyle and an insane number of earrings, gave me a Marlboro Light. "Sure," she said. Then she lit it for me. "Are you here all by yourself?"

"No," I said, inching away a little. I hadn't really meant to strike up a conversation or anything. "My friend is just a douche bag who left me standing here."

I looked over at Noah, and the three of them followed my eyes.

"Noah da Stonah?" one of them asked.

I rolled my eyes and sighed, exhibiting the embarrassment I didn't even realize I had. "Yes."

But they didn't laugh at me. "Does he charge you?" the tall one asked. "I bet he doesn't. Are you guys fucking?"

Seriously, it's not like I'm a prude or something, but I almost fell over. It was just so out of the blue, you know? I don't even really curse that much. Plus, gross. "No,

God," I said when I got my voice back. "It's not at all like that. But no, he doesn't charge me."

"She's hooking up with that freckled guy," another one of the girls said. "Suzanne Fisher's little brother."

The other two leaned back and said a long "Ohhhhh" together.

"No, really, we're not," I replied, putting up my hands, and I accidentally dropped my cigarette. "Shit!"

"It's okay," the tall one said. "Here, take another. I steal them from my mom anyway."

"Thanks," I said as she lit a new one for me. "I'm sorry."

"Don't even worry about it."

When I put my cup to my lips and nothing was left, I realized I'd been very quickly draining it as I stood there.

"Um, I'm going to get a refill," I said, happy for an excuse to make myself scarce from this conversation. "Thanks again for the cigarettes."

"No problem!" they said together, waving. After I turned around and had walked a few steps away, I heard them laugh a little and then go back to a loud but unintelligible conversation.

Noah found me at the keg. My second beer was already half drained. "Simon's not coming," I said when he walked up to me.

"Which is what I told you," Noah replied. I looked down and noticed he was rolling a joint. "Stick out your tongue."

"Gross," I said. "Lick it yourself."

So he shrugged and licked the paper and sealed up the joint, then twisted the ends. Then he handed it to me. "Your honor."

I took it off him and he lit it for me as I puffed at it.

"*Hold* it, Lily!" Noah said, accusingly, like I'd never smoked a goddamn joint before. Seriously, the tiniest puff of unsmoked smoke escapes your lips, and Noah is ready call the goddamn pot police or something.

I held the hit a few seconds and let it come slowly out my nose—more blood vessels that way, according to Simon. The three senior girls were watching us. I made eye contact with the tallest one. After a second, they were walking over to us.

"Can we join you?" the tall one asked. "Let's go over there, though," she added quickly, gesturing to the corner of the yard, behind some old playset, "so we don't, you know, attract attention."

"Whoa, come on," Noah said. The girls just sort of cooed at him. His shoulders slumped, but he couldn't say no. So we split this joint between the five of us, standing in the deeper shadows at the corner of the yard.

"Lily," Claire said. That was the tall one, with the earrings. She was much taller than me. Her hair was blacker than mine, too. "You need another beer."

I think we must have been at the party for a couple of hours at this point. These girls were having a goddamn blast playing Get the Sophomore Wasted with me, but

I didn't mind. If Simon wasn't going to show, I might as well make the most of it and get completely plastered—that's how I saw it.

Claire and I traipsed back to the keg. The tap was gone, and a crushed cup sat on top of it.

"Oh, no way!" Claire shouted, at pretty much the top of her lungs. "Aaronson! The keg is kicked."

Kyle—or someone who decided to act as proxy—called back from somewhere in the yard. I barely caught it through the din: "I know. There's a run ongoing, chill out."

Claire didn't seem in any mood to chill out, however. Instead, she crushed the cup in her hand and threw it down. "This is an outrage!" she said, thrusting a finger in the air. "I paid my five dollars!" Then she stomped toward the voice. I think. And she thought, I imagine. I doubt she was seeing or hearing any clearer than I was, really.

As she reached the steps off the deck, though, she slipped, and fell onto the lawn. Her two friends laughed their heads off, and I did too, and Claire rolled around on the lawn. As she got to her feet, she vomited.

"Oh, gross," Noah said. He had been standing next to me. I didn't know for how long. "Listen, we should go."

"Fuck you, Noah," I said. "You go. We're having fun."

"You're gonna stay here with these three?" Noah asked, shocked.

"So what if I do?" I said. My heart suddenly jumped, like I'd been having some ongoing hypothetical argument, one I knew for sure I'd lose in the real world. Quickly I reminded myself the matrix had shut down for the night, and I felt better again.

Before Noah could reply, we heard sirens. An instant later, there were red and blue lights flashing from over the house, in the front yard.

"Shit," Noah whispered. "Look, I have to go, right now. You can do whatever you want."

So I went with him. He started toward the front yard, and I grabbed his wrist. "Moron," I said. "You want to walk right into them? Come through the back."

I pulled Noah with me right into the shrubs at the back of the yard. Behind Kyle's house was the water tower, and on the far side of that was another cul de sac, which led down to Centre Drive. From there getting to my place would be a short walk.

As we walked under the water tower, I was still holding Noah's wrist. I stumbled on something, and he caught my hand as my butt hit the cement.

"Ow."

I looked up at him. He was staring down at me. I don't think he was drunk at all. I didn't look Noah in the face very often. But he looked pretty cute to me right then.

"Are you okay?" he asked. I was still holding his hand, and he held out his other to help me up.

"Yeah, I'm fine," I said. I found that if I squinted a little, his nose shrunk, and he looked a little—enough maybe—like Simon. "I—" And I realized I was crying.

"Get up," Noah said. I took his hand and he helped me up. We walked the rest of the way to my house in near silence, with me leaning on Noah quite a lot. I was still crying, but also laughing. I never would have guessed I would be the one who would need help getting home from a party. Especially with Noah.

"Did you sell all your weed?" I asked. It was pretty out of the blue.

"No," Noah replied. He didn't say anything more until we reached my house. My mother's light was on upstairs, but the proctologist's car wasn't there. That was nice.

"He's not here," I said.

"Who?" Noah asked.

"Never mind. I'm home. Thank God. I feel awful."

We stood in front of the door as I dug around in my pocket for my house key. It took a little while to get it into the keyhole, but I managed, even with Noah pawing at my hands and saying, "I'll do it, drunky." He was smiling at me. He thought I was a fool.

"I'm fine!" I exclaimed as I pushed the door open and fell inside. "Just go home, okay?"

Noah took my wrist and I spun to face him. "What?" I snapped.

And then he tried to kiss me. I swear, it caught me completely off guard, and for an instant his lips were on mine. It wasn't a kiss, though—not really. My upper lip pressed against my teeth, which hurt, and I was trying to say "What the fuck" the whole time. Finally I just pushed his shoulder and he backed off of me.

"Noah, are you kidding me?" I said. "What the fuck was that?"

"A kiss, Lily!" Noah snapped back. "A fucking kiss. Or it was supposed to be. Sorry it wasn't up to your goddamn majesty's standards."

"'Standards'?" I shouted at him. Clearly, any chance of getting to bed without waking Mother was pretty well shot. "That wasn't even a kiss. It was more like assault with a disgusting mouth!"

"Fuck you, Lily, okay?" Noah replied, which I guess I had coming. "I'm sorry I'm not Simon, is that what you need to hear?"

"Shut up, Noah," I said. Suddenly I was meek. "You're a moron."

"Really?" Noah said. "*I'm* a moron? Who's the moron here, Lily? Because as far as I can see you've been lusting after Fisher since you were like twelve or something, and he barely even looks you in the fucking face when he graces you by saying 'hey'!"

I went and sat on the bottom step and put my face in my hand. The tears tasted like salty beer. My mother called down, "Lily? What is going on down there?"

Noah wasn't finished, though. "Let me tell you something about Simon, okay?" he said. "Because I know about guys like Simon. He doesn't feel about you like you feel about him, and if you hang around long enough to get him to think he loves you, you'll regret it later."

Now he was done. He walked through the still-open front door, and I jumped up and slammed it behind him.

"Lily? Answer me this minute. What is going on down there?"

"Nothing!" I shrieked up the steps. "Just go back to bed. God!"

Mom was standing on the landing watching me then, in her robe. She looked like hell. It was two in the morning. "We're going to have a long talk tomorrow, Lily," she said very calmly. "I'm not happy with the way you've been acting lately."

"Fine!" I said, and I stormed into the first-floor bathroom and slammed the door and flicked on the fan to drown Mom out. Then I threw up.

| chapter 8 |

For three years, I'd been trying to hold on to Simon and pull him up against me. He was a bar of soap in the shower, though: slippery as hell, and one false move—squeeze a little too tight—and he's gone. And picking up a wet bar of soap in the shower is pretty difficult.

It was November, and I was at Noah's house, in the bathroom off the kitchen, brushing my teeth. I was beginning to see a little more clearly, having just puked my guts out, and with them about four cans of beer and most of my bong buzz. Those Mary Janes of mine seemed farther and farther away. I mean, it was a *Thursday*; I don't know what I was thinking. But the hypothetical argument creation matrix can make me do anything, some nights.

Noah's bathroom floor, by the way, is tiled in huge sage and cream squares and hexagons, respectively. There are thirty-eight complete tiles, plus eleven cut tiles. There's a small crack on the huge mirror over the sink, in the corner. Right in the front of the crack is a soap dish. Most people probably wouldn't notice it. But Lily Feinstein, having locked herself in the bathroom after being sent off by a wounded Simon Fisher, wondering how long to stay locked in, will amuse herself.

This wasn't much of a party, which was fine—it's not like I wanted to go to another open-house kegger in this lifetime. Especially not with Noah. But Noah had apologized like crazy for that night after Kyle's party, and I forgave him; what choice did I have? Then, when he asked me to come over, even with Goody and Hilly there already, I went. The hypothetical matrix was in full effect, and this time I was sure Simon would be around. He took forever to show up, though, so I had a lot of time with nothing to say, and with people I didn't want to be around, with which to smoke and drink myself sick.

And now I was dying of alcohol poisoning and Simon was lying on the kitchen floor in a pool of his own blood.

I'm being dramatic. But he was on the kitchen floor, and he was bleeding. Goody finally attacked him, for real. That guy had been a dick to Simon forever, but I guess they couldn't take both being at Noah's house at the same time. It was either they fought, or the universe exploded. I don't even really know what sparked it. Like I said, I was pretty fucked up.

When I'd been on the bathroom floor, hugging the toilet, I heard Noah's front door slam, and Simon shout "Fuck you," so I was pretty sure he hadn't moved from the kitchen floor. I had no idea whose toothbrush I'd picked up, but I'd cleaned it in some very hot water before using it. I'm sure it was fine.

I flushed the toilet and stood at the door waiting for the whooshing and refilling to finish. Then I opened the door and walked down the hall and down the steps to the basement TV room. No one was around, so I just dropped onto the floor and flipped through the channels on the TV. The water was running in the kitchen, and after a few minutes it was quiet. A moment later, Simon came in. He was holding a dish towel against his nose. It was pretty well stained with blood.

"You okay?" I asked.

Simon shrugged. "What about you?" he asked. "Do you feel better? I heard you retching in there."

"I'm fine."

He sat down next to me and put the towel on the floor. "Your nose is still bleeding," I said, and I reached up and touched the blood on his upper lip. My finger exposed his big freckle, the fake bloody lip I noticed three years before. It was lighter now.

"I don't feel a thing," he replied, and then we were kissing.

I was still drunk, and still a little high. His lips didn't feel close enough, somehow—not right away. My hand found its way to the back of his neck and I tried to pull him in tighter. I could taste his blood, and it was delicious. I know that makes me sound like a psycho or a perv or something, but it really was.

Simon's legs were out in front of him, and his back was against the couch, so I pivoted and straddled him and we kept kissing like that. His hands moved between my ass and my rib cage on my back. I couldn't help myself; I was completely pushing myself against him, and it was amazing. Then Noah walked in.

I jumped off Simon immediately. I must have been about as red as a baboon's butt just then.

"Hey, don't let me interrupt," Noah said. And he walked off. I couldn't tell if he thought it was hilarious or tragic or if he was about to go kill himself or what. But I slid against the couch and let my hand play on Simon's neck. He kept his hand on my waist. Suddenly he seemed nervous.

"Are you all right?" I asked.

"Why do you always ask me that?" Simon said. He sighed.

I tried to backtrack. "Should I leave you alone?" I asked. The bar of soap was slipping.

Simon shook his head and pulled me to him, and we kissed again. I felt a wave of relief wash over me, and threw my arms around him.

"I'm really tired, Lil," he finally said. He was drifting off right in my arms. "I'm going to sleep in the guest room."

I slid back to let him get up. "It's Thursday, though," I said. "You're sleeping over on a Thursday night?"

He shrugged. "My parents won't care," he said. "Good night." And he walked off toward the old maid's room.

Simon and I met in seventh grade, like I've said, about a hundred times, I guess. But none of that mattered, not until one day that December. It must have been one of our last practices for winter track, or maybe even one of the first for the spring team. Who can tell the difference?

Jake and Hank and I were pretty much thick as thieves by this point. The three of us were clustered together by the infield fence, laughing like hyenas, when Simon strolled into the infield, into the milers' stretching territory. It was cold, and his sweatshirt hood was up over his baseball cap. All our hoods were on; from afar we would have all looked the same.

Melanie jogged to meet him at the gate from the track. "Hey, Simon," she chirped.

Jake and Hank and I watched the two of them. We three weren't smiling. It felt cool. I almost wanted to light up right there, just for the effect, but I didn't have the guts. So we just glared, and I was satisfied with the cold-weather vapor I pushed from my lips.

They talked a minute or two. With my hood on, and with the wind picking up, I couldn't make any of it out, and I couldn't clearly see Simon's face. Jake took my hand and I squeezed his, kind of for luck, I guess.

I guess Robin got tired of standing alone and stretching while Melanie flirted with Simon. He walked over to them. I saw a nice huff of steam shoot from his hood as he stomped over. Simon's head dropped as Robin and Melanie talked for a second. Melanie was angry, maybe at Robin. I don't know.

Simon stretched on the fence and Robin walked over to us three freaks.

"Simon Fisher is running with us today," he said. He puffed out his chest a little bit and looked anywhere but right at us: the trees on the far side of the football field, the tennis courts, back at Simon and Melanie, just not us. "On the street course. He says he's not much of a long-distance runner, so he'll probably be toward the back. Help him not get lost out there, okay?"

We three nodded, and Robin jogged off to start the run. Melanie joined him after a quick word to Simon, which I also didn't catch.

"Shall we?" Jake said to me. He still had my hand, so I followed him and Hank.

Simon jogged after us. "Hey, wait up."

Hank turned to face Simon, but walked on with us, backwards. "Don't bother following us, Si," he said. It made Simon sound like an old man or something. "We're not running the course."

"I know," Simon replied. He caught up to us and started walking next to me. "I'm not here to run the stupid street course, man."

The four of us just walked on like that, toward the daycare center. Jake and Hank exchanged looks about a hundred times, and at some point Jake let go of my hand. When we stepped onto the grass near the swings, Jake gave me a cigarette. I pulled out my own lighter—it had been Hank's, but I liked it and he let me keep it—and lit it.

Jake and Hank went over to the seesaw and sat together on one end, and I settled into a swing.

"Can I have one?" Simon asked. He was just standing there.

Jake and Hank—another glance. Then Jake took out a cigarette and lit it and passed it to Simon. He had no idea what he was doing with it.

"You don't smoke," I said quietly. Simon sat on the swing next to me. Both our hoods were still on, but I could see his face now. He looked so pale, and his eyes were red where they should have been white, and under his eyes it was puffy and dark, like he'd been in a fight. "Are you okay?"

Simon didn't say anything. He didn't even really look at me. He just swung a little and puffed on the cigarette. The smoke coming out was white/blue, though, so I knew he wasn't inhaling anything.

"First pull it into your mouth—just a little," I said. "Like this." I took a little drag.

"Then, take a deep breath." I took the smoke all the way in and then let it come out my nose.

Simon coughed till he was red in the face. The cigarette fell from his fingers into the dry, worn patch under the swing.

"Your boyfriend is wasting my cigarettes, Tiger Lily," Jake called from the seesaw, singsongy.

"Fuck you, Jake!" I singsonged back.

Tears ran slowly down Simon's cheeks, and it took all my will not to jump from the swing and take his chin in my hands and kiss him all over his face. I wanted to taste his tears.

"I'll go," he said. He got up.

"No!" I got up too. "We'll share mine. It's no big deal. Jake is just kidding."

"Right!" Jake called over. He and Hank were on opposite sides of the seesaw now, using it like you're supposed to. "I'm a big kidder."

I walked to Simon and stood about an inch from him. In the cold, I could feel his breath and the heat coming off his face. "Here."

I held out my cigarette carefully, so he could take it without burning his fingers.

"There's lipstick all over it," Simon pointed out.

I looked down and laughed. A ring of crimson circled the filtered end.

"It doesn't matter," he said. He took it awkwardly and put it to his lips. After a small puff, and a small inhale, he let out a tiny cloud of smoke. "How was that?"

I laughed again. "I think you got it," I said, but I was looking at his lips, where a tiny trace of my lipstick had managed to grab on.

I sat there for a while, on the floor of Noah's TV room. I could still taste Simon's blood.

There was some happiness in my chest, but not much— not enough. I expected to be over the moon, or something, but I wasn't. I was definitely scared, and confused, and feeling a little bit of a rush when I recalled the kiss—when I thought about sitting on his lap, straddling him and pushing myself against him; I had to catch my breath. But it wasn't . . . finished. It was like half-cooked chicken: made me sick.

The light in the old maid's room went off, but the door was still open a little. I got up and tiptoed down the hall. Noah was asleep on the couch in the first-floor TV room. The TV was still on. I felt like a cat burglar, the only person awake in a house that wasn't mine.

When I reached the maid's room, I heard Simon breathing, very slowly—asleep. I pushed the door open wide so the light from the hall fell over the tiny twin bed. The blanket was up over his head; only his arm stuck out and hung over the edge of the bed. I walked over and stood there, looking down at this lump under the cover, for a few minutes. I could have just walked home pretty easily and picked this whole thing up in the morning, or even after the weekend. Whenever.

But like I said, half-cooked chicken, and I already wanted to throw up. So I carefully peeled the covers back, like the top of a yogurt cup, only under here was Simon in his T-shirt and underwear, and there probably was no fruit at the bottom.

He groaned a little and rolled onto his side to face the wall. I pushed off my sneakers and undid my belt, which made a huge racket, and let my jeans fall to my ankles, then quickly slid into bed too. He was facing away from me, so I curled up behind him and buried my face in the back of his neck. My left arm I put over his body, and he took my hand and said, "Hmm."

"It's me," I said. I kissed the fuzzy short hairs. Simon turned a little and we started kissing. He pushed himself against me and I held onto the back of his neck. His hand slid down my back, and he let his fingers slide just into the elastic of my underwear. I pushed my hips into him, and felt that he was hard.

Nothing more happened, but all my doubt was gone, and I woke up happy.

| chapter 9 |

Track has two seasons: winter and spring. Oddly, winter starts in fall, while spring starts in winter. It's best not to overthink it.

At one of the first meets of my seventh-grade spring season, I was hanging back during the mile run with Jake and Hank, as usual. If I'd been slow before, you can imagine how two months of smoking had not improved my speed. We were about halfway through our second lap of four, and Melanie had already lapped us once.

"This is fairly sad," Jake pointed out.

"Rather," Hank agreed. I gave them a short "ha." When we started our third lap, Robin passed us too. He had stopped shaking his head in disappointment before the winter season was up.

"Come on, Siegel," Freeman shouted from the infield. "You're lagging. Don't lose speed now!"

Jake, Hank, and I twisted our necks to watch Melanie as she slowed down—she'd really hit a wall—during her last lap. A couple of runners from the other school, not to mention Robin, passed her with plenty of time. Then the three of them kicked and raced for the finish. Melanie didn't even finish in the top four.

"Think we can catch her?" Jake said with a twitch of his eyebrows.

I shrugged. "I don't think I want to make the effort to find out," I said.

Hank patted me on the back. "Atta girl."

We finished—eventually—with the slackers from the other school right beside us. We ought to start our own league of sad smoker track slackers, I thought. Together, Jake, Hank, and I walked over to our bench.

"I think this pretty much settles it, Melanie," Freeman was saying when we got there. "You have a really strong start, but you don't have the stamina. So we're giving you a new place on the team for the new season, at least until you can work on your endurance."

Melanie was bright red, mostly from the cold and running herself into the ground, but I hoped a little embarrassment was mixed in there too.

"First of all, you're joining the 200s," Freeman went on. I glanced at Simon, who definitely perked up at the name of his event. "We need another body in that event anyway."

"I really don't like short distance, Mr. Freeman," Melanie said.

"Normally, you know, I let everyone run what they want," Freeman said. He put a hand on her shoulder. "But you're a strong short-distance runner; I think you could do very well."

I swear, Melanie looked right at Simon. He looked back at her.

"Okay," she said. "I'll do 200s then."

"Bah bah bah!" Freeman said, putting his hand up. "That's not all. Second, you're staying on the mile, too. But you'll be our rabbit. We've never had one, but it might be fun, and I think you'd be great for the position."

"Rabbit?" Melanie asked.

"You'll run just like you are now, maybe even faster off the start," Freeman explained. "With any luck, the hot shots on the other teams will try to keep pace with you, while Robin keeps a steady pace behind. It'll tire the other guys out."

"So, I'm like . . . bait?" Melanie asked.

I put my hand over my mouth but let a giggle slip. She glared at me a second.

"Call it what you want," Freeman said with a shrug. Then he walked off and started scribbling in his clipboard.

Jake put a hand on Melanie's back. "Tough break," he said.

Melanie just threw him off and sulked over to the Gatorade.

"Touchy," Jake said. But I wasn't paying attention to him anymore. Simon had joined Melanie at the Gatorade, and in half a second they were laughing.

New Year's Eve, sophomore year.

Mom had been out of town, with the asshole specialist, and she'd left me on my own.

I brought in Simon's favorite takeout, and I had candles set up and everything. It was supposed to be a romantic night; for weeks now, when I closed my eyes I always saw our first night sleeping in the same bed at Noah's. I thought I was ready.

I heard a car in the driveway and ran to the window. Suzanne was driving, and she and Simon sat in the car talking for an eternity. Finally she gave him a kiss on the cheek and he climbed out. Naturally, I scurried from the window and opened the door. Simon stood there, holding a paper bag, in his baggy sweater and jeans, with his sad eyes and lip-snarl freckle, and suddenly I was scared—nothing seemed right. I just felt like a stupid kid playing dress-up.

Then Simon's sister Suzanne had to give us both a heart attack, even though she'd already driven away.

Simon held out the paper bag—a bottle of champagne. But Suzanne had also slipped a condom into the bag and it dropped out of the bag and landed on the entryway floor. We both just stood there, gaping at it, like morons poking a dead raccoon with a stick at the side of the road or something.

I threw it away.

Then I ran back to the living room and blew out the candles, and we ate dinner in front of the TV. I finally felt better, and we made out a little, but the real fun part, just so the year would go out with a fizzle:

Between ridiculous horror movies, Simon said, "I'm going to join track again, I think."

He went on about smoking less, running more, and I felt the soap slip just slightly out of my hand.

I was overreacting, wasn't I? I mean, I have my hypothetical argument creation matrix for a reason, right? And sure, it kicked into high gear when Simon left in the morning on the first of the year. I didn't see him until we got back to school after break, though. Simon's dad had gotten sick a little before the holiday break, and now he was always busy with family stuff.

But my HACM fixed everything for me: Of course Simon joined the track team. His father was sick, so Simon figured he'd better get himself healthy, for its own sake but mostly for his dad. The hypothetical argument, for your enjoyment:

"Simon joined track?" Noah asked in disbelief. "That's retarded."

"I know, but it makes sense." I'd already won that argument, you see. "He's on track again to make his dad happy. His dad was way into running track when he was in high school. That's all there is to it."

Noah, fully convinced, never raises the issue again. Thank you!

Getting back from break is a pretty horrible experience, I think probably for everyone. For me, it was maybe especially disgusting though: Ms. March practically pounced on me when I walked into her homeroom.

"March seventeenth," she said. Her painted nails (cherry red) dug into my forearm.

I looked around. Luckily, no one else had noticed our Math Goddess's descent into madness. "What . . . about it?" I asked.

Ms. March tossed her hair out of her face, briefly slapping me across mine with it, and sighed. "Lily, the Fair is on March seventeenth."

"Ohhh," I said, nodding. "Okay. I'll keep it in mind."

"Keep it in mind?" she said, obviously aghast at my lack of enthusiasm. "You've got to commit to this thing. Tell me I can submit your name to the committee."

So I shrugged. "Okay."

Ms. March shrieked and finally let go of my arm. "Good. We should meet about your presentation. I smell a blue ribbon!"

I smell a psycho math teacher.

"When can we meet?" she added quickly as I turned toward my seat. "It will have to be after ninth period, if you can do that."

Since quitting track after one day of it in ninth grade, I haven't had any—*any*—extracurricular activities. But if I planned one with Ms. March, I figured it would give me a great reason to be hanging around the school when Simon got done with track practice at four thirty. Done.

Or we can check in with HACM and determine in fact that my reason for agreeing so readily was to improve my standing with Ms. March, make me look better on my college apps, and, of course, my love of the aesthetics of mathematics . . . or whatever.

"Today works for me," I said.

"Excellent," Ms. March replied. "Lily, I can't tell you how happy I am with your performance in my class this year. It's such a turnaround from last year." The start-of-homeroom buzzer sounded. "We'll meet in the math lounge, right after ninth."

Elijah's foot was waiting patiently for my ass three seats back, so I walked down the aisle and sat down. He leaned forward.

"Hey, Feinstein, I heard you're finally putting out for your boyfriend Fisher, that fucking nut," he said. "Do they allow conjugal visits at the hospital's psych ward?"

I spun to face him. "Tell you what. If you don't get your foot out of my ass, I'll break your leg and you can ask the nurse at the front desk when you get wheeled past to the ER."

"Ooohh," he moaned. But he did move his foot, and then cackled.

What? He made me angry. It had been almost two weeks since New Year's Eve, and I just wasn't seeing enough of Simon, so when fucking Elijah went and asked about him—even calling him my boyfriend, which was the first time anyone had done that with any semblance of accuracy—I guess I overreacted a little.

Our first day back was a cold Monday, but after meeting with Ms. March for an hour, I decided to take a route around the back of the school, past the track, on my way to the front door to wait for Simon. I walked right up against the school, where the black sidewalk is, across the soccer field from the track itself. No one would have noticed me, not from up on the track—possibly even from right on the sidewalk with me, but I digress. The point is I wasn't spying, really. But I could pick out Simon well enough. Even from that distance, picking out the redhead among all those brown-haired Jewish boys isn't too hard. Once I spotted him, I thought I'd be sick: he was hanging out with Melanie. Even after three years watching her, I still could hardly believe it.

While I stood there, struck immobile with shock and disgust, Simon collapsed onto the infield lawn—that'll teach him to join track again after the year and a half we've had together. Melanie was immediately by his side, leaning over him, with her bleached hair falling all over the place. Then he took her hand and got up. For every instant, every tiny fraction of a second, that his hand was in hers, my stomach got tighter and tighter. Finally he let go and went to the starting blocks, and I was able to walk again, though barely. I reached the front door as my step count hit 372, and I sat on the curb, surrounded by all these other goddamn idiots, yapping and yapping and ignoring me—not a complaint—and took out a cigarette and lit it. I didn't cry.

"You don't have to wait for me," Simon said when he walked up. The sun was already low by then, and everyone else who'd been hanging around was long gone. I was on my fifth cigarette, though, hugging my knees. I'd taken off my pea coat and held it over my arms. I was wearing my Kittie T-shirt—the one I never would have bought if not for his CDs, and his dragging me to a concert—over a thermal, and I wanted Simon to see it. I wanted him to be hurt by it.

I shrugged and stood up. "I know. I was meeting with Ms. March about this math thing I have to do." I gave him a kiss hello, then held out my pack of cigarettes. "Want one?"

He didn't ask what math thing, or why a meeting with Ms. March would last until the fucking sun went down. He only asked, "Where'd you even get those?" Like I couldn't ever have my own pack.

"Noah gave them to me." Which he had, that morning. Yes, I felt weird about it. Simon had been a no-show, and I guess Noah was moving in for the kill or something. Whatever. He tried once, and I was pretty clear; there was no on-leading happening.

"Did you two smoke up together or something?" Simon asked. He seemed kind of annoyed. In fact, he didn't even look me in the eyes; he just turned away and started walking toward 25A.

I got to his side. "Hey, what is your problem?" I snapped.

"I don't have a problem," he shot right back. "I just didn't want a cigarette, okay? I'm trying not to smoke, and you know it."

Yeah, I knew it. I also knew . . . "I was watching you at practice today."

Simon looked down at the pavement and tightened the brim of his hat. He has quite a few tells; play him in poker and you won't regret it, I suspect. "Yeah?"

"Do you like that girl?" I asked. I choked on the words a little. Pretty disappointing; I'd been happy so far that day with my kick-assness, but I guess it had gotten too heavy.

"What girl?" he asked, but I noticed he didn't look up. He knew who I meant, which made his answer pretty irrelevant: if she was already on his mind, the answer was yes, whatever he said.

"Melanie Siegel," I said. It came out bitchier than I'd intended.

Simon stopped. "No." He finally looked me in the eye.

I looked back, hard, and said, "Really?" and then I started crying. It started with one tear escaping past the little Dutch boy, but then it was over.

"Really."

I threw my arms around him and prayed in my heart that we would put his around me, and he did. I sobbed into his neck and shoulder. Thinking back on it now, I'm not sure why I was crying; either I was relieved to hear him say no, or I was already mourning the end around the corner. With an active HACM, always running in my head, it's impossible to know for sure.

| chapter 10 |

This is how it ends.

She'll worm her way between you, slowly, always smiling, so even when the break really hits, you won't be able to feel anything anyway. You knew it was coming, even before she did. Before she knew you existed.

And you'll be walking with your second-string boy across the athletic field. You've just had your last-nerve meeting with the Math Goddess, and she's sure you'll win in the sophomore competition at the Math Fair in a couple of months. But you won't even show up, you know this now. Things are going to be far too black by then.

The sun is going down, over the Hills—your neighborhood—past the tennis courts, and the track, and the daycare center, and you'll think about Jake and Hank for a split second. Then there's laughter. You'll take one more drag of your cigarette, and Noah will suddenly take your hand and squeeze it: *Look.*

He's looking past you, so you'll turn to look too, and you'll see your boyfriend running across the grass, smiling—he never smiles at you, it seems lately—and holding hands with the girl you always knew would be the one. You've known since you were twelve.

Your heart will stop, and you won't cry right away, but you'll look down at your shoes, wet and muddy, and realize *these* are your shoes—the Mary Janes are far too small now. Noah will lock eyes with you when you can look up, and when you thought he might care—when you thought he had a decent bone in his pot-addled, self-centered brain—"I told you."

And he'll turn away from you and let go of your hand. Then he'll light a menthol and walk off, because he was happy to see you fall.

Because this story was never about you, anyway. One. Two. Three. Four. Five. Six. Seven. Eight. Nine. Ten. Eleven. Twelve. Thirteen. Fourteen. Fifteen. Sixteen. Seventeen. Eighteen. Nineteen. Twenty. Twenty-one. Twenty-two. Twenty-three. Twenty-four. Twenty-five. Twenty-six. Twenty-seven. Twenty-eight. Twenty-nine. Thirty. Thirty-one. Thirty-two. Thirty-three. Thirty-four. Thirty-five. Thirty-six. Thirty-seven. Thirty-eight. Thirty-nine. Forty. Forty-one. Forty-two. Forty-three. Forty-four. Forty-five. Forty-six. Forty-seven. Forty-eight. Forty-nine. Fifty. Fifty-one. Fifty-two. Fifty-three. Fifty-fo

| part two |

NOAH

| chapter 1 |

All the fall days sort of blur together: Simon, Lily, weed, the Gap. A little blood.

But the Gap. This new girl had just started working at the Gap in the fall.

See, in our town, there are two malls. One is nice and indoors and has a goddamn Abercrombie and Fitch or whatever the fuck so it stinks to high fucking heaven like cologne all the goddamn time. The other mall is the shit mall—a strip mall. It's got a goddamn grocery store in it. And that's where the Gap is.

It's also where we sit on the curb, Lily and Simon and me, smoking cigarettes and just sort of talking things over. Anyway, we used to.

This one afternoon, I don't know, before Thanksgiving for sure, Simon wasn't around, which at this point was pretty weird, but it works out well because you need to know about me and Lily first.

It was pretty cold that day, I guess, and me and Lily were sitting on the curb outside of the Gap. I wasn't wearing a coat, though, so I got up and bounced a little, just to get warm.

Simon is always saying I act like a cokehead. But he knows I don't do coke. I know everyone probably thinks I do. Everyone can eat it, though. I'm a little hyper. ADHD or some fucking thing. Who cares, right? So diagnose me.

Lily looked up at me. She has these big brown eyes. It sounds corny, but they totally get me. They make my stomach and heart flip five times a piece. So I looked away quickly, because I have a tendency to kind of stare at her if I don't catch myself. It's been like that forever. Well, since I met her, anyway. When she catches me staring I feel like a complete douche. She always calls me on it, too.

"Man, it's cold," Lily said.

"Yup," I said, continuing to bounce for warmth. I kept my eyes on my sneakers. "You need to get up and move."

"No way." She huddled in tight, pulled up her knees. She looked really cute. "Noah, why did your family leave California? I'd kill someone to be in California right now."

"Who? Who would you kill?"

"Anyone. Name him. . . . Or her."

I thought about it for a second. I could have said my dad. His fat face popped into my head pretty quick. That seemed pretty depressing, though. I wasn't looking for pity from Lily.

"My dad." What the hell. Why not.

Lily just chuckled very politely, though.

"Come on, get up and bounce," I said, trying to kind of change the subject, get her mind off my dad and that whole fucking can of worms I just didn't want to start opening. "It'll keep you warm, and I'll get to see those beautiful boobies bounce up and down."

"Noah!" She was probably really offended but I just sneered a little and laughed.

Lily really does have the biggest tits in our school, I'm pretty sure. She's had glorious fucking tits forever, though, far as I know. Soon after I first moved out here from Cali, in the middle of seventh grade, someone told me she paid for them.

It's obviously bullshit. Even in this town girls aren't buying tits at age thirteen, right? But they really are that fucking glorious. Still, she hates when I talk about them. Dudes are endlessly telling her how great her tits are, and it drives her crazy. I don't know why, honestly. If girls came up to me in the halls and shouted, "Hey, giant-cock man!" I'd be loving that shit, for real.

Tits, that's what I was about to get into. The new girl at the Gap had very nice tits. Not huge like Lil's or anything. But really nice. I had this thought that I'd like to get my hands on them.

I turned to the Gap window and looked in. "New girl working at the Gap," I said to Lily. "I'd like to get my hands on her tits."

Lily rolled her beautiful eyes and put her chin back on her knees. "Big shock."

The truth is I don't get any action from the ladies at all. None. I'm not going to try to hide this immutable fact from you. But you also have to understand that if I didn't spend so much time with Lily and Simon, I'd probably have a better shot.

I'm not stupid. I know Simon and Lily are a couple of the biggest freaks in school. But they're my best friends, and I'm in love with one of them. Besides, Simon is pretty much my best customer.

I should probably mention that I sell a little bit of weed. Now and then.

"Why do you have to *constantly* talk about boobs?" Lily asked.

I stepped off the curb and then back up. Repeat. "I don't *constantly* talk about boobs."

"You do," she insisted.

I don't. Not constantly. But I had a plan. It hadn't worked, obviously, but the plan was, if I kept letting Lily know how much I'm a boob man, she'd pretty soon realize I was the man for her, right? Clearly I would fully appreciate her particular attributes.

"Where the fuck is Simon?" Lily said.

I should probably also mention that she was totally wet for Simon. Only Simon never seemed to realize this. The school at-large assumed they were married already with seven children or something.

"I'm cold. I'm going home."

She got up and turned to face me a second. I looked away as she half bowed good-bye.

"Bye, Noah. Tell Simon I left."

"Yeah, I think he'll figure that out pretty quick when you're not here."

She gave me the finger and walked off. I watched her walk away and cursed her pea coat for covering her ass.

What? I'm not *strictly* a boob man. It's not like I'm religious about it or something.

That afternoon, Lily wasn't going for my boob strategy at all, as you can see. I glanced into the Gap, then pulled my cigarettes from my back pocket and lit one. (They're menthols; I can smoke and have fresh breath all in one shot.) I figured I'd wait a minute to see if Simon was going to show up at all. It was after five, so I was pretty sure he'd come and gone already, before Lily and I even got there. This was back when Simon never hung out past five on weeknights.

But whatever. I was in no hurry at all to get home. At home there are exactly five things that interest me at all, and four of those are televisions. The other is dinner, when it happens, which is pretty rare.

Plus the one thing you can pretty much bet on, my dad will be home, sitting in his office at the back of the house. He'll be puffing away at some nasty cigar, screaming into a goddamn phone, watching six finance networks.

Once in a while he might stick his head out to shout at my mom, or to call me a goddamn faggot.

Wanna come over?

My dad moved us out here about three years ago now. We'd been living in Orange County out in California, which was fine with me. But it wasn't fine with someone, because my dad left his medical practice, sold the house in about a week flat, and shipped me and Mom off to Long Island, New York.

Unfortunately for me and Mom, he followed a few weeks later. I don't know what he was doing still in California for those few weeks, but I have a feeling it wasn't dishing up holiday meals at a shelter for battered women, or anything charitable like that.

Soon after he got to Long Island, he put his hairy arm around my shoulders. He'd been at his new practice all day, and now he was home; his sport coat was off and lying on the back of our new black leather couch in the music room. His shirt sleeves were rolled up past his elbow, and I could smell a day's worth of cigar smoke and BO. His silk tie was loose at the throat.

I had been looking at this hideous painting he'd had hung in the living room. (Yeah, had hung. As in, my dad doesn't pick up a goddamn hammer and nail to hang his own painting. There are people whose fucking life calling is to hang shit up, move shit around, change lightbulbs, whatever.) It was one of five paintings in a collection he had shipped from some artist in Oregon. Who knows how much they cost him. Must have been hundreds of thousands, from the treatment they got. They showed up one morning with two armed guards. They're still up in the house today.

Anyway, each one features a mermaid, playing a harp or peeking from behind a giant clam shell or just looking generally slutty-coy. You can't see any tits at all, but my mom hates them, I'm pretty sure. I don't blame her.

So I was standing in front of one of these new paintings. All the living room lights were off, except for the five spotlights he'd had installed to shine directly on each of the mermaid paintings. "Noah," he said to me. "Noah, do you like this painting?"

I shrugged. I wasn't even thirteen, not quite the smart ass I am today.

The douche bag pulled a fat cigar out of his shirt pocket and jammed it into his mouth. Then he went on, talking through his teeth like Spider-Man's boss at the fucking newspaper.

He squeezed my shoulder. "You know what this painting is?" he asked. He pulled a lighter from his pants pocket and sparked it.

Careful, I thought. *The booze on your breath might blow us all to Kingdom Come.* Two years down the road, I was saying shit like that out loud. But for then, at twelve, I just looked at my feet and said, "A mermaid?"

He let go of my shoulder and slapped the back of my head in one smooth motion. Not too hard, but I must have jumped. I know I said, "Ow, Dad, what the hell?"

"Whoa, whoa, sorry, Nancy," he replied with a smirk. "So sensitive. Take it easy."

He took a deep breath and sighed, then muttered under his breath. He pulled his tie off and tossed it onto a nearby recliner.

"It only looks like a mermaid," Dad went on. He took a short puff off his cigar. "In actuality, this is Glenn Lerman's BMW."

"It is?" Glenn Lerman was one of Dad's partners back in California.

Dad nodded, then placed his hand on the back of my neck and squeezed for a second, then let go. He walked over to the darkest corner of the living room and I heard some glass and ice clinking. Must be a banner evening; his third scotch, and not even six yet.

Dad laughed and took a good swig from his tumbler, then moved over to a different mermaid painting. This one was a redhead mermaid, looking over her shoulder at you and smiling. She wasn't smiling at me, though. She was smiling at Dad. Their smiles seemed right together.

"This painting here," Dad said. He gestured at it with his drink. "This one is that asshole Jerome Preston's condo in Laguna Beach." Another partner.

I glanced at Dad, then chose another mermaid, pointed at it. "What about that one?" The minute I said it,

I regretted it. My voice sounded shaky and off. He would think I was mocking him.

Dad swirled his glass. The ice clinked around a little and he drank the rest in a single gulp. Then he looked square at me. His face was suddenly hard and serious.

I stared back for an instant, but looked back at the painting.

"That one?" Dad said, looking into his glass, hoping an ounce was still there. "That's Aaron Roth's little girl, her goddamn college tuition. I don't know. Where's your mother?

"Cheryl!" he called out, much louder. "Cheryl, we're out of scotch again!"

With that gem, he walked into his back office and closed the door. Mom's reply, that a delivery would be coming in the morning, was quiet, timid, and unheard by the man in the house.

| chapter 2 |

November. I spotted Simon Fisher strolling down Cardinal Drive, like he does every morning. Pretty much every day since we met in science class when I first got out here, me and Simon have walked from Cardinal to school together. We've come a long goddamn way since then.

"'Sup, Fisher!" I called out from up the block. He could barely be bothered to look up, of course. I swear, sometimes that dude is the walking fucking dead.

Simon pulled the headphones off his ears and dropped them around his neck. "Hey."

Know what's fun? When your morose douche bag friends are insisting on shoegazery douchebagitude, really amp it up. Get loud, jump around a little more. . . .

"High-five me, bitch!" I said. Excuse me: fucking exclaimed.

Simon managed to lift his hand, which must have weighed about seventy pounds.

"Dude, you are not a morning person, do you know that?" I pointed out.

"How can you be so awake at this hour, man?" he asked me. Then he looked at me. "Wow, dude. Nice shiner."

I reached up and felt around my eye. It was a little sore. "Eh, it's not that bad," I said. And it wasn't. I mean, I had pretty much forgotten it was there. But my dad and I had gotten into it pretty good the night before, so there it was.

"I don't want to talk shit about your dad or anything," Simon said. Which of course means he's about to talk shit about my dad. "But I'd call the fucking cops if I were you. Your dad's a class-A prick."

I shrugged. I know what Simon thinks. He thinks my dad beats me, like it's child abuse or whatever. But it's really not like that. The thing is, we *fight*. You can believe that dude has to show up at his office sometimes and tell a bullshit story about taking an elbow to the face in a pick-up basketball game over the weekend. But I did that. I gave him that black eye, or that bloodied lip.

For now, he's still giving it back twice as good, though.

I just said to Simon, "If I was gonna turn the dude in it wouldn't be for this black eye, dude, believe me."

Look, I won't sugarcoat it. I know my dad's a fucking prick. He treats my mom like shit, he treats me like shit. . . . He even treats the partners at his medical practice like shit.

Still, he's not exactly my favorite topic of conversation, so I changed the subject. "I've got some excellent trees for you in this bag of mine, Mr. Happy Pants."

"Oh yeah?"

See, that's what perks this dude up in the morning: my weed. He is never as happy to see me—or Lily, for that matter—as he is to see some weed. Not that I blame him. I mean, he sees me every fucking day, and this was some very good weed.

"Yeah. Do you need to make it to first period today?"

Simon cocked an eyebrow at me. "Define 'need.'"

See what I mean? Mood shift, 180 degrees. "That's what I'm talking about."

The back of the high school came into view as we turned onto Hill Crest, and there was Lily, slumped against the maple tree behind the tennis courts.

"Lil-*yyy*!" I called out. My goddamn mating call.

Simon shushed me. "Come on, Noah. It's seven thirty in the fucking morning. Can we respect the sanctity of me being fucking tired?"

I shit you not. He really says shit like "sanctity" all the time. He also writes poetry. *Poetry*. He doesn't know I know, but I know. "Sorry, sorry."

Lily got to her feet, but it wasn't me she was happy to see. "Hey." She gave a half wave, with her elbow bent, and her hand below her shoulder. Then she shoved it right back into her pea coat's pocket. A second later she pulled it back out to push her hair behind her ear. It was a windy morning.

It wasn't too windy for Simon, though, our resident bowl packing, wind guarding tour de force. Before I could even say good morning and get comfortable, he was passing me the bowl and coughing his lungs out.

I laughed. "You like that?" I asked him. "Cough to get off, my friend."

Simon nodded and coughed his ass off.

"Are you going to Rohan's class?" Lily asked him.

"Nope," Simon said. She was sitting up against the tree, and he was leaning on her, like she was a goddamn easy chair or something. I stood up and took the bowl from him, then handed it to Lily without taking a hit.

"Ladies first."

Lily leaned around Simon and took the bowl from me with one hand and pushed her hair out of her face with the other.

"It's too windy," she said. "I can't . . . Simon, light it for me?"

Simon was on cloud nine though, and I'm quicker anyway. So I leaned over and lit the bowl for her while she held her hair and covered the carb. She took a pretty small hit and held it, then blew it across Simon's face.

"What the fuck, Lily?" he said. She laughed and threw her arms around his neck.

I reached into my back pocket and pulled out a cigarette and lit it. I wanted to vomit. You're probably thinking, Why the fuck does this guy hang around these two? Or step up and be a man, or whatever. I don't know. This was every morning, practically. Three days a week, I bet: I sit down, stand up, sell some weed, smoke some cigarettes, and watch Simon and Lily flirt each other's pants off.

That particular morning, Lily mentioned some open-house party happening. She pretty much begged Simon to go with her, and he of course ignored her. Lily ignored me, though, when I expressed my bubbly goddamn enthusiasm. Then, since Simon had skipped Rohan's class, when the haze started to lift it was almost second period. Lily and Simon have that class together. Which left me, lying on my back on the lawn. I lifted my head, strained my goddamn neck, and watched them walk off until they were out of view.

My head dropped with a quiet thud on the hard, cold dirt of the schoolyard. I rolled my head to one side and saw the tennis courts. They always remind me of back home in Cali, where everyone I knew had a court or three on their property. I took lessons for two years out there.

I rolled my head away from them and saw my cigarette butts, dirty and bent, all smoked right down to the filter. There were seven of them. I knew they were all mine, all clustered together, there; Simon smokes some shit without filters, fucking nut; Lil smokes whatever she can get, usually what she bums from Simon, but there's always a load of blood-red lipstick on her butts, so they're easy to identify.

Simon was the first friend of mine to come over to our new house. It was a weeknight, and after dinner, after seven, I think. The sun was down, and I was hiding in the basement.

Not hiding like a kid in a closet, afraid of the boogeyman. Just kind of keeping out of the way, playing my Xbox or whatever. The basement had already been turned into my TV and game room. Dad had his own room, in addition to his office, which had two TVs and a sweet sound system; that was on the second floor. Mom had her own room, too, that she called the solarium. It didn't have a TV, but it had speakers mounted all over the place that piped in music from Dad's system in his room. In other words, the house was arranged so we could spend as little time as possible with each other. For that reason, it also had a goddamn intercom system. When we first moved in, I loved that. I was constantly slapping myself in the chest and going, "Mr. La Forge, why have we stopped?" and shit like that. I'm telling you, I was a total fucking moron.

Starting that evening, though, that goddamn intercom became my bane, my absolute arch nemesis. When Simon rang the front door buzzer, I took the steps two at a time to make sure I beat my mom to the door.

He was standing there with his big sister, Suzanne, who must have dropped him off. She looked a lot like him—reddish hair, freckles, all that—and was kind of hot, which was a combination that was a bit troubling, honestly. Simon was in baggy jeans, with safety pins in them here and there. His black T-shirt had a huge skull on it, and he was wearing it over a shirt with long sleeves. Now I'd seen everything.

"Hey, Simon," I said.

"This is Suzanne," he said, without looking at either of us. "Bye, Suzanne."

She laughed and gave him a hug and kiss on the cheek while he screwed up his face at me. "Bye. I'll be back in three hours."

She started down the path back to her car in our driveway, walking sort of backwards. "Nice to meet you, Noah!"

"Come on in," I said to Simon.

"Who's there, Noah?" my mom called from the solarium.

I closed the door after Simon stepped inside. "Take your shoes off, okay?" I said, then I called over my shoulder. "Just a friend from school, Mom. For a science project."

That's when the goddamn intercom crackled into life. "Is it a girl?"

Simon looked at me. I looked back. I couldn't talk.

"Are you a girl?" the speaker asked flatly.

"Um, no. I'm . . . not."

The speaker laughed. "Of course you're not. Because my son is a homo."

"He's kidding," I said. Simon glared at me. "No, he's really kidding. He's got a terrible sense of humor, my dad."

"He's an asshole," Simon replied as he kicked off his shoes. "So what do you know about molecules?"

"Dude."

The voice was far off, but it kind of woke me up. I'm not sure I'd actually fallen asleep, but I was deep enough in my head so it wouldn't have made any difference. One thing I know for sure, I was still on my back, and staring straight up at a mostly clear sky. The clouds were hurrying across the blue. I heard the flag in the front of the school flapping. I heard trees shaking, and right over me I saw the maple tree Lily loved. Its leaves were completely changed for the fall, but they hadn't done much falling yet.

"Today will be the day," I said quietly. "Windy day like this, no way they're going to hold on."

"Dude." This voice drawled over the lawn. It was Danny Goodman, I could tell, and he was getting closer. There aren't too many people who would (A) come looking for me in the middle of second period, and (B) know where to look: under a goddamn maple tree. Not to mention the goddamn announcement: "Duhhhhooooood," immediately followed by a very throaty laugh.

He sounded far away still. He had probably come out the back doors, spotted me, and immediately duded from all the way across the field. The goddamn back doors must be like a hundred yards from where I was.

"Hey, Goody," I called out without getting up. "What's up, dude?"

Danny Goodman. If one man smokes more weed, buys more weed, and talks more fucking shit about Early Girl and Northern Lights and Swiss Miss than yours truly and Simon Fisher, it's definitely Danny "Goody" Goodman.

The sound of his shoes on the grass got closer, and soon he leaned over me and smiled right in my goddamn face. "No, dude."

"No" is short for Noah. It's not "no."

"Ha ha, you're flat out, dude," he said. His breath smelled like a goddamn breakfast sandwich. . . . with sausage. "How fucking high are you, No?"

I looked up at his smiling, weakly bearded face. "I was looking for you yesterday. Do you think I enjoy carrying around a fucking ounce for you the whole day?"

He laughed. "Where is it, dude? I have money today."

"All right, back up off me a little, you faggot." He laughed again, but stood up straight and backed up so I could stand without knocking into his face.

"Follow me to my locker, all right?" I said, shaking my head. He saluted me and walked next to me toward the back door. "You and Hilly should come by this weekend, man, by the way."

"Oh yeah?" Goody asked. He was barely there, his mind totally on the ounce in my locker.

"Yeah," I said. "Bring Kyle too, if you want. More the merrier. Mom and the asshole will be away all weekend— some trip out west. But I just got the new Madden, and Hilly's been psyched about it."

"That's cool," Goody said.

Listen, I know Goody and Hilly are kind of douche bags. But to be honest, they get laid a lot. It's only fair that I, as the person who supplies their weed, should get some of that action. It's not like they're such bad guys, anyway, and I'd been thinking a lot about sort of ditching Simon and Lily, once in a while, like I said.

The halls were pretty quiet, but not empty or anything. The seniors rarely go to class. Typically, if a senior has already missed homeroom twenty times—yes, twenty—they only show up for that, and ditch everything else. There's no point in going for them. Most of them have already had their transcripts sent off to the college of their choice anyway. Unless they get wait-listed or something, no school will ever care how they do in high school from this point on.

Of course, that's not to mention the people in every grade that cut regularly, including yours truly. Goody and I walked down the central hallway, and people were huddled in little groups near the library, or at the big windows off the snack bar, or on the handicap ramp by the gym entrance. Some people nodded hello or didn't look up at all, or a group of girls laughed so you'd want to vomit— but whatever caused it, this thought crossed my mind: I don't belong out here with these people; I belong in my goddamn remedial math class, which I could ace with one hand tied behind my back, so I could get on with my life, turn eighteen and get out of here and never look back.

But I shook it off, like I always do. And I opened my locker—15, 39, 22—and reached up to the back of the top shelf and pulled out a paper bag and handed it to Goody.

He swung his backpack around and jammed the paper bag inside.

"And bring some chicks, okay?" I said.

"What?" Goody mumbled. He pulled his canvas wallet out of his backpack; it had a cheesy picture of a sunset on it and said "Aloha!"

"If you come by this weekend, bring girls."

He laughed. "Right, dude." He paid me. "You know it." As he turned away, he slapped himself in the forehead. "Man, Aaronson's party is this weekend. You should come by that."

"Oh right," I said. "Planning on it."

"Bring some product, too, 'cause I know that dude will buy," Goody added. "Probably half the damn varsity team would."

Then he put out his hand, and snapped my fingers. "All right, dude. I'm out. Peace."

Goody turned around and walked through the front doors, out to the traffic circle, where Hilly was sitting on a railing with Megan Zaretsky.

Goody grabbed Hilly by the arm, and Hilly hopped down, reached for Megan's crotch, and laughed. Megan laughed too, and Goody and Hilly walked away. I heard Hilly shout, "Later, ho," and my face got hot. I didn't know who I wanted to punch in the fucking face, but it was someone.

By the way, me and Lily went to that party at Kyle Aaronson's place. I'm not getting into that whole mess, though.

| chapter 3 |

Everything at home went to shit in December. It was a Wednesday.

When I got home that afternoon, there was broken glass all over the floor in the entrance. I looked down and saw my face looking back up, but in slivers on the hard marble floor. All that was left of my mom's antique mirror was the silver-plated frame, still on the wall, crooked.

I called out to her: "Ma? What happened?"

She came out of the kitchen, shuffling, with her head down. She was holding a dustpan and brush, and she immediately got on her knees at the broken glass.

"I'll do it, Ma," I said. I joined her on the floor and tried to take the brush from her, but she wouldn't let me.

"I'm fine, sweetie," she said. She looked down at the pile of glass so her hair fell over his face. "It's no big deal.

I knocked the mirror with my shoulder and it broke. I can clean it up myself."

"That's bullshit, Ma." My mom didn't "knock" shit. The only knocking that went on was compliments of Dear Old Dad, I assure you. Specifically, he knocked his wife and the mother of his beloved son into a wall, and the mirror got in the way.

I tried to push Mom's hair out of her face and she turned away from me, but I saw that she had been crying.

"Noah, please," she said with a little laugh, like I was overreacting or something. Like it was possible to over-react in our house. "And keep your voice down, will you?"

That made it pretty obvious that Dad was home and on a fucking rampage. I heard a TV go on in his office.

"Why is he home so early?" I asked. Dad usually stayed at his office pretty late. He and his partners would sit around in their lounge smoking cigars and watching the financial news. Anything beats coming home to this place, I guess. Anyway Dad was usually home at seven at the very earliest, and here it was not even four.

My mother sighed and relaxed her shoulder. Then she reached up and pushed her hair behind her ears.

"Your father's former partners back in California are suing him." She put an arm around me, like I'd need com-fort after hearing this earth-shattering news.

"What took them so long?" I replied. I almost smiled.

"Noah, I know you have had your differences with your father"—understatement of the fucking millennium, by the way—"but this is very serious. Your father could lose his practice."

Seriously, I couldn't give a shit about his practice. Hell, if Dad ended up getting totally reamed, I was all for it. But I also knew that when the world fucked Dad, Dad took it out on Mom.

So I left my mom there in the entryway, slipped down the basement, called the cops, and called my grandma in Bellmore. You don't need to hear all that dialogue. Just believe it wasn't fun for anyone. But that was that. And about four hours later, the house was empty—Dad was at the police station, Mom was at her mother's—and I had the place to myself.

I decided to throw a goddamn party.

| chapter 4 |

I didn't go to school the next day. Instead, I was up until four in the morning, rolling godfathers out of my dad's twenty-dollar cigars and crying like a bitch, if you want to know the truth. The minute I woke up the next afternoon, I hit the basement, flipped on the Xbox, and lit one of those godfathers. By the time the doorbell rang that night, I was out cold on the couch. I woke up to the incessant buzzing of the front door intercom and the occasional pound on the door itself. The Xbox was cycling through the annoying music and cut scene it plays if you don't start a new game. My eyes were dry as hell. I leaned over and hit the button on the phone.

"Who is it?"

"No, dude," the phone crackled back. "Open the door, you moron."

"Seriously, dude," the phone added in a second voice. "We've been out here for days ringing this stupid bell."

"It's cold!" the first phone voice added.

"Okay," I mumbled to the phone, and I rolled off the couch and found my way upstairs and opened the door. In my state, I half expected to see the basement phone standing there, bigger than life, hugging itself to keep off the chill.

It was just Goody and Hilly. They barged in, pulling off their ridiculous Sherpa hats.

"Finally," Hilly said. "What the fuck, Noah? Were you jackin' off or something?"

Goody thought that was completely hilarious. "You do look pretty out of it, No."

The two of them made themselves right at home, hitting the fridge, pulling glasses out of the cupboard. Hilly had his head in the pantry when he called out, "Noah, do you have any chips?"

We didn't have chips, and the plate Goody was using to reheat a slice of old pizza in the microwave was a meat plate. He might as well have taken a shit on the lambskin rug in my dad's office. But whatever. That asshole wasn't coming home soon.

I ignored everything Hilly and Goody were doing, and asked, "Just you two?"

"Who did you expect?" Hilly replied. He'd found some cold chicken and was eating it out of the Tupperware, which at least wasn't soiling the goddamn house.

"I thought you were going to bring some girls." I tried not to sound whiny, but I think I did. "Some *ladies*," I added to cover.

Goody laughed. "*Ladies!*"

Hilly shook a drumstick at me and practically shouted—with his mouth full, spitting everywhere— "Dude, think about what you just said. What 'ladies' do you think are going to jump at the chance to hang out at casa de Noah da Stonah?"

"Whatever, Hilly. You idiots are stoned more than I am."

Hilly stared at me. "But we also rule the JV football team and get mad cheerleader tail. You just smoke."

I held his eyes for a minute, felt my face get hot. The microwave beeped and Goody jumped up from the table to retrieve his pizza.

Suddenly Hilly's face broke and he laughed. "Dude, relax," he said to me. Then he dropped the Tupperware into the sink. "Is there beer or what?"

Goody took a huge bite of pizza and said, "Basement fridge, am I right, No?"

"Yeah, basement," I said. "Help yourself. I'll be down in a minute." And I grabbed the phone and took a seat at the kitchen table. First I called Simon, but there was no answer.

"That fucker better show up tonight," I mumbled to myself, then I dialed Lily and stood up. She answered on the first ring.

"Hi, Noah."

"Hey, Lil," I said. I walked in a circle around the kitchen table. "You coming over tonight or not?"

"I guess so. Who's there now?"

"Um, just Goody and Hilly. They're tearing my house apart."

"Sounds like fun."

"You have to come over. Simon will be here soon and if you're not here too Goody and Hilly will probably kill him with their bare hands. They hate that guy, you know."

Mostly I had to drop Simon's name to get her off her ass. I know how things work.

"Yet another reason for me to *not* be near those guys. Why do you even like them?" She sighed big. "Okay, I'm on my way. See you later."

"Cool. Bye, Lil."

I put the phone down and looked at the open basement door. The sound of the Xbox reached the kitchen table, along with the smell of my weed no one had paid for. I sat down again and slumped, let my head hang back so I was looking across the room upside down. My dad's office door was closed, locked, most likely. Behind it was the good scotch, two leather chairs, an oak desk, a flat-screen TV, two computers, a sheepskin rug. But the best part, the part that really defined my dad—defined me—was the seething hate and the violence, and that we stashed neatly *under* the rug.

I was almost fourteen the first time I hit my dad. I guess I'd like to say I did it in a moment of passion, like I was blind with rage or some shit. *That was one injustice over the fucking line, Pops!* I might have shouted. But really, I'd been thinking about it for years. My dad had never hit me, he'd never done much more than dropped these little nasty comments on me, like calling me a homo in front of my friends, or muttering under his breath that when he was my age, he was spending every weekend knee deep in snatch.

I'm his son. I don't know why he liked making me feel like shit, but he obviously did.

So I fantasized a lot about hitting him, making him cower, making him bleed from his nose. It didn't go down like that at all.

I was sitting at the kitchen table one night, not doing anything. The lights were off, and I was just sitting and listening to the house. Mom was in the solarium, hiding out. Dad was in his office. I could hear his TV, on the financial news channel. I could hear him get up every so often to refill his drink. Once he walked past me—right past me—to refill his ice bucket. God forbid he have room temperature scotch. Or say anything to his son sitting in the dark kitchen.

I waited a little while longer, sitting in that kitchen chair, leaned forward, tapping my feet, flexing my fists. I had counted five scotches, and after the first they had probably all been doubles. He was good and drunk. My mother's music, piped into the solarium, was Beethoven's Ninth—conducted by Leonard Bernstein; she listens to him constantly—and a crescendo would cover for me as I pushed open Dad's office door and found him leaning, his elbow on the mantle of his gas fireplace, his head hanging. The only light in the room came from the blue flames and the TV. Dad's glasses were on his desk, on a stack of papers. His eyes were closed.

I stepped up to him, and his voice rang in my ears, though he didn't say anything. I heard him laugh quietly like he does. I heard *homo* and *faggot*, and I saw the crinkle of his eyes when he smiles at me with no love, only scorn. I heard my mother crying out, crying so hard that her chest heaved and she hiccupped and coughed.

I gritted my teeth and faced him, and he had no idea I was in the room. The chorus of the fourth movement was belting out German praises to the Father, and I muttered, "I hate you." Then I hit him. My fist struck his left cheek, and it hurt—my hand stung then throbbed, and Dad shook awake from his trance. "Ode to Joy" soared through the room as Dad turned to me and wiped his cheek. His eyes crinkled as he looked into mine and the corners of his mouth turned up, just a little.

I don't know what I thought. Maybe that he would go down like a sack of flour, drunk as he was, and just pass out—forget the whole thing, but I'd have a nice, fuzzy memory. Instead I got a broken nose and started a war.

I didn't get up from that chair until Lily rang the buzzer. When she did, I groaned and went for the door.

"You look like shit," she said.

"You look fucking ravishing," I replied, because I'm very smooth like that. She stuck out her tongue and pushed past me. At the top of the basement steps, she stopped and turned to me.

"Simon's not here?"

I shrugged. "Not yet. Have a beer, relax."

"I'm not going down there with them."

"Why not?"

"Because they're mean jerks, and I don't want to."

I put a hand on her shoulder. "Well, that's where the beer is, and that's where the weed is. And anyway, they're my friends."

She looked at me sideways.

"Just come on. Don't be a baby." I gave her a gentle push and we both went down. I don't know what she was worried about. Seriously, Lily is not the type of girl these guys care about. They barely looked up when she walked in and took a seat on the floor. No one even said hi. I went to the fridge and took out two cans of beer.

"Beer me!" said Goody. "Also your weed is shit. Where's the good stuff, dude?"

"Fuck you, Goody," I said back. But I got him a beer.

"Hello," Hilly said without pulling his eyes from the TV. That was his nice way of reminding me he, too, required beering.

I shouldn't put up with it, but I do.

For an hour, Lily sat at my feet on the floor in front of the couch. Goody and Hilly eventually gave up on the Xbox and switched to flipping through the channels, looking for Japanese game shows. They just got higher and higher and drunker and drunker. Goody even paid me for the weed.

Lily and I split a bowl and several beers. She got pretty fucked up, even let me play with her hair. Laid out on the couch, with Lily's head so close to mine, and my hand in her hair, I started thinking maybe she'll forget about Simon. Beer could do that. Beer and weed could definitely do that. But Goody piped up.

"Dude, Lily, aren't you Simon Fisher's girlfriend?"

Lily was shocked. Aghast. Not really.

"No, I'm not. We're just friends."

"Well your *friend* Simon Fisher is a fucking nutcase." Hilly howled at that.

"Shut up, Danny," Lily said.

"Yeah," Hilly chirped in a high voice, "shut up, Danny."

But it was over for me. She sat up and moved away from my hand. Eventually the buzzer rang. Simon decided to grace us with his presence after all.

The crowned prince of sadness was in rare form. His Yankee hat was lower than usual over his eyes, which were more bloodshot than Hilly and Goody's put together. He wasn't acting high, though, so I assumed he'd been weeping over some poetry or something. He took off his coat and dropped it on the floor, then headed down to the basement. Of course, he took the seat I'd had, right on top of Lily. She looked up at him like he was Jesus Fucking Christ.

I'm a total fucking champ at keeping my chin up. Seriously. Two of the biggest douche bags in history lounging in my TV room, and the girl I daydream about, looking longingly at my best friend—do I get down? Angry? Nope. I'm the host with most.

"Take a hit off this," I said to Simon. This was the good stuff, too. This was the stuff Hilly and Goody came over for. This is the stuff I kept aside, and packed into my best bong—three feet long. But Simon wasn't interested.

He should have taken that hit, though. Just one hit. Because Goody decided if Simon wasn't here to puff, then Goody was going to start some shit.

Apparently they'd run into each other that morning, and Simon was being a freaky weirdo. You know, himself.

"I was just telling your girlfriend what a nutcase you are, Fisher," Goody said.

It had actually been an hour or more, but we all stretch the truth now and then, right? Not me, though. Promise. I mean, why bother?

"Fuck you, Goody," Simon replied. He leaned back on the couch and pulled his hat down over his face. "You're a fucking moron."

Goody laughed. "What did you say?"

"I said, 'Fuck you, Goody,'" Simon said again, slowly. He sounded pretty choked up. I knew right away where this was going. I grabbed my three-foot bong and moved it out of harm's way.

Just in time, too. Goody could have housed Simon in a fair fight, like in the schoolyard, high noon, both of them in their best shape—that is, less high than that night. But as it was, Goody was stoned to the rafters and drunk as a skunk. He never even made it to the couch. Instead his feet got tangled in my Xbox cables and he tripped into the coffee table.

Simon looked up and laughed, which was the wrong choice. Not that there was a right choice. And in Simon's defense, Hilly was laughing too. But Goody was extra pissed now. Simon was smart enough to use these few moments to get out of the room. He jumped up from the couch and made it up the basement steps. I hadn't seen him move that fast in years.

"You're dead, dude," Goody said as he jumped over the table and made for the stairs. Lily shrieked, but we were all sort of laughing at this point. Not for long.

I followed Goody up the steps, calling after him, "Let it go, Goody! He's just being an idiot."

But he didn't listen. He caught up to Simon at the entrance to the kitchen.

"Don't you fucking turn your back to me, dude," Goody said. He was seriously pissed off. It occurred to me I'd never seen him not smiling, at least a little. Even on defensive line that guy was goddamn Smiley McGee. I guess the lesson is, don't kill a dude's buzz, especially if he has the most tackles on the JV football team.

Simon turned to face Goody, as per his command. Stupid move. I know Simon pretty well. I mean, as well as anyone else knows him, right? This kid cannot fight at all. Facing the onslaught of Danny Goodman wasn't going to work. If it were me? Keep walking, to the kitchen table, and sit down. Very calm. I know I don't seem that way, but I can be very calm when I need to be.

Simon wasn't calm, though. When he turned I caught a look at his face and he was a mess. Even Goody stopped for a second, inches from Simon. Fisher's face was bright red; his eyes were still completely bloodshot.

Goody muttered, "Dude, you okay?"

Simon just stood there, like a cartoon stack of TNT: the plunger is down, the charge is down the wire, and the dynamite is throbbing—the only thing stopping it from blowing is the poor sucker sitting on it.

Simon didn't answer, at least not in so many words. He just took a swing. I don't know what Goody had been feeling—second thoughts on hitting the crazy crying guy; fear of the pent-up anger inside the crazy crying guy; who knows—but when Simon's fist connected with Goody's nose, and Hilly said in my ear, "Well, that was a long time coming," all hesitation went out the window. The football star did what he does best: tackle. I heard Simon's head hit the floor, like a fucking bowling ball.

Goody was on top of him when I stepped in and grabbed his arm. "That's enough, Danny."

"We should go, Danny," Hilly said.

Simon lay there, eyes closed, for a few seconds. Long seconds.

"He's fine," Goody said, and he gave Simon a little slap on the face and got off him.

We all stood around Simon. I swear I didn't even breathe. Lily stood behind me, as if Simon might finally blow and send shrapnel in all directions. Goody was right over Simon, right at his feet, so Simon looked like Goody's reflection on the kitchen floor.

Goody kicked Simon's sneaker.

Simon smiled.

"Asshole." Goody kicked his shoe again. "Insane, loser, asshole."

Lily finally came out from behind me and was at her wounded soldier's side in an instant, practically in tears.

"Come on, Danny," Hilly said. His coat was on, and he was holding Goody's. "Let's just go, okay?"

Goody took his coat and waved us off. "You're a bunch of freaks." And they left. Goody slammed the door, and as it hit home, Simon shouted, "Fuck you!"

I turned to him, lying on the floor, blood dripping from his nose. "Man, that's fucking *Breakfast Club*."

"Fuckin'-a right it is." He smiled again and got up on his elbows.

"Here," I said, handing him a beer. "It's cold. You could use it."

Lily put a towel on his head and he just shook her off. "I'm fine. You don't look so good, though. You must be drunk as hell."

Lily dropped the towel and went into the bathroom off the kitchen, probably to bawl her eyes out, thanks to Simon being such an asshole. Simon just opened the beer and drank it.

Meanwhile I picked up the towel and wiped up Simon's blood drops from the goddamn kitchen floor. Simon kept slurping at his beer. I finally said something. "Dude, what the fuck is wrong with you?"

He didn't answer. Just sat there, drinking that fucking beer on my kitchen floor. His blood dripped down his chin onto his shirt, and he didn't even look down. When I left him there, with that question hanging between us, he didn't even look up. Just straight ahead.

I went and watched TV in my dad's lounge. After a little while—maybe about twenty minutes—it was pretty quiet down in the kitchen, so I prowled down there, just to see what was going on. The light was on in the basement and the bathroom off the kitchen, but there was no one in there. I went in and cleaned up a little, then shut off the light to check the basement. I sort of figured after that fiasco, Lily and Simon would have just gone home. But I hadn't heard the front door close or anything.

I headed down the basement steps, and then stopped in my tracks. I'd found Lily and Simon: Simon was on the floor, leaning against the couch, and Lily was on his lap, straddling him, grinding into him like a fucking stripper doing a lap dance or something. She was kissing his neck, and his face, and running her hands all over him and shit. Simon meanwhile had his hands on her back and ass and everywhere else.

So I stood there, just watching them, still in the darkness of the stairwell a little, and I felt something wash over me. At first it was pretty painful, like I'd been kneed in the groin. But then it got sort of warm and tingly and spread into my chest and my shoulders and down my legs, and I felt like I weighed nothing at all.

I stepped into the light and Simon saw me. Lily suddenly turned, then jumped off his lap. So I smiled, big, like a moron. "Don't mind me!" I shouted at the top of my fucking lungs, and I turned right around and went back upstairs.

I slept on the couch in my dad's lounge. Lily and Simon slept in the guest room, in this little twin bed. I hope it was miserable and cramped. They shared a glass of orange juice in the morning, and Lily got in the shower. Simon sat next to me on the couch. I was curled under this ugly blanket. It had a huge picture of a black cat on it. The TV was on, and this gorgeous morning-show blonde was going on and on about all the relatives we'd have to put up with during this wonderful, joyful holiday season.

"Not me," I muttered under the blanket.

She smiled at me, and made a joke about house guests and fish.

I looked her in the eye and said, "Fuck off," and she smiled back at me, all teeth and lips. The camera cut to a wide shot, and now she was legs and tits, and teeth and lips.

Lily was still in the shower; I could hear the water running through the pipes. I closed my eyes and pictured her, standing in the steaming bathroom, letting the water run over her. Maybe she was using my soap.

But she was Simon's legs and tits, and teeth and lips, like my mom was my dad's, and like Hilly and Goody had their sets all over town.

Simon got up from the couch and I smiled a little as he left the room. Somewhere in his future, maybe there was a fifteen-year-old son, twisted in the basement, and maybe he'd lay him out.

| part three |

Cancer is a darkness that
grows and grows and
eats Good for breakfast.

I have two
and one is in my head.

When the two meet in my chest,
The Good will crawl
Into a corner of my heart
To die.

SIMON

| chapter 1 |

God, I wish there was somewhere to shop in this town besides the Gap.

For as long as I can remember, I've gone to the Gap just before the beginning of each school year for new clothes. When I was little, I went with my mom. For a couple of years, Suzanne took me shopping. With Suzanne gone, I went by myself. Sophomore year, I was a little late, and it was halfway through the first week of school before I finally dropped by. I didn't even need anything, really. Maybe a pair of jeans.

After I just stood by the front door for a few minutes, trying to figure out which rack was the guys' jeans, this beautiful girl came over to me. She was wearing those tight tan pants, the ones that don't reach the ankles.

Looks ridiculous, but that's all right. I don't think this girl could look terrible if she tried. I struggled to lift my head up, but when I saw her chest I decided to just stare at my feet instead. "Do you need help finding anything?"

"No, I'm just looking," I muttered, turning away. I headed for the nearest rack and flipped through some shirts. Ugly shirts—just awful. That girl eventually headed off to annoy someone else, and I made my way to the jeans. In a few minutes I was at the register. It doesn't take long to pick out a pair of pants.

The girl at the register didn't even look at me. She just grabbed the jeans and started in. "Hello!" Very chipper.

The cashiers at the Gap have these scripts they have to read when you get up to the counter I guess. An effective business strategy: employees who behave like vacant robots will encourage sales. Okay.

"Would you like to save ten percent today by applying for the Gap card?"

The Gap card. I cocked my head to one side and pulled some bills from my pocket. The cashier finally looked up. "How old are you?" she said, and her mouth twisted and spat like she was sucking a lemon peel or something.

"I'm fifteen," I said. I tried to throw the "no kidding, twit" accent in there, like Suzanne does so well. Not sure she picked up on it.

"Oh, you're too young for the card."

I know that. It's a real shame, too. I can't wait to get a Gap card.

"So does that mean I can't get ten percent off?" I said with a smirk.

"'Fraid so," she said, handing me my receipt and change.

I grabbed the bag from the counter and headed for the door. As I walked past the socks near the front, keeping an eye on the cashier, I knocked a pair or two into my bag and kept moving. There's my ten percent, sweetie.

"Bye now."

Jesus, I nearly shit my pants. I spun around, practically tripping over the mat by the door. It was that damn girl with the chest being ultra-friendly to the customer.

I almost couldn't speak over the sound of my heart doing flips in my chest. Not sure if that was the shock or the tits, really. "Bye." My lips said it—I felt them pull apart. I'm just not sure my voice backed them up. I was looking right in her dark eyes. I started to feel sick.

"Nice socks." She raised her eyebrows at me and turned away with a smile. For a minute, I watched her walk to the back, and then I moved quickly out the door. I lit a cigarette as I reached the path to my neighborhood on the other side of the parking lot and sat down for a while, thinking some very nice things about the dark-eyed girl. After I finished my cigarette and popped a piece of gum into my mouth, I headed home.

On the way I saw this neighborhood kid, about eight or nine years old I guess. He stuck his tongue out at me, then ran up his driveway and hid behind some garbage cans. I smiled at him and took a heavy step up the driveway. He shrieked and ran into the garage. I wasn't going to do anything. I mean, I was only screwing with the kid. Truth is, I just wanted to play with him, I guess. That's like the best age. That's when your big sister takes you by the hand everywhere, and you're her pride and joy. My sister once looked at me like that, a long time ago. My sister used to be my whole world.

My sister used to say you should hold your breath and cross your fingers when you drive past a cemetery, so I always did. There's this one along the Long Island Expressway in Queens that must be about five miles long.

"You're both going to pass out," my mom would say.

We never made it the whole way. I'd give out first, usually, and start breathing again with a gasp and cough. I guess Suzanne just had bigger lungs. She also had this way of raising her eyebrows at me that meant, "Nice try, loser."

My parents used to take Suzanne and me to Manhattan a few times a year, probably more than that. We'd stand in line in Times Square to get half-price tickets to some or another Broadway show. I never really developed much of a taste for that stuff, but I remember some good times, too. I was obsessed with *Annie*. One of the girls in the orphanage—Pepper I think she was called—was probably my first crush. She had these long braided pigtails and really dark freckles all over her face, and she was sort of the tomboy tough girl. Just really cool. I must have been about six.

The last time Suzanne came along we went to see *Into the Woods*. That one was very good too. I don't think I had any crush on Little Red Riding Hood, but I wouldn't rule it out. And the next day, Suzanne left for college. She turned seventeen the same day. I was almost thirteen. I sat in her room as she finished packing. I guess I'd been crying.

"It's a good thing you've had me around, Simon," she said, mussing my hair. "Most guys your age would never cry."

"Screw you." I kept my eyes on my feet and tugged at my socks.

"Fine," said Suzanne, tossing another bag onto her shoulder. "Whatever." A car horn. "That's my ride. Do I get a hug good-bye or what?" Dad was calling from the bottom of the stairs, so I gave her a quick hug, and she kissed my cheek. "I'll see you soon," she said, and I remember I just stayed there, sitting on her bed and sulking until the sound of her ride got quieter and then vanished. I never even looked from the window.

| chapter 2 |

My mother was already in the kitchen making dinner when I got home, carrying my blue-and-white Gap bag and chewing my wintergreen gum. She heard me come in and called to me.

"Where were you?" There was no anger in her voice, but I could hear her bracing herself for an argument she was sure would follow. One usually did if I took that long getting home from school, but not that day.

"I just had to buy some jeans," I called back, starting up the stairs to my room. I wanted to get up there and maybe beat off before dinner.

"Can I see them?" Great. She needs to see them, be the interested parent. They're fucking jeans.

"Mom, they're just jeans," I said, but I stopped and went to the kitchen anyway, immediately dropping the bag on the counter and sitting down at the table. I just didn't want her to hug me. She'd smell the cigarette, and we'd get into it again. Would've been the worst time, too. I mean, I could handle a fight with my mom, but with my dad it was different. He'd always seem so fucking disappointed. It was more than I could take, and he'd be home any second.

"Simon, these are exactly like the ones you're wearing now."

"Those are the ones I like."

"Why don't you get a variety? What's the point of having eight pairs of the same jeans?" She dropped the jeans back on the counter and started stirring something.

What's the point of having a variety? What's the difference? "What's for dinner?"

"Mac and cheese." Well that's good, anyway.

"How much time do I have?" I asked, heading out of the kitchen.

"Not more than ten minutes!" That's plenty. I couldn't stop thinking about that girl at the Gap. I was thinking I might have to start buying a lot of jeans. Of course, that's not all I was thinking, so I did what I had to do and washed up for dinner. I reached the bottom of the stairs just as my dad was coming in the front door.

"Hello." He always shouted "hello" the moment he walked in. It was half general greeting, and half "where is everyone?"

"Hey, Dad." I gave him a quick hug and pulled away; I figured the smell of cigarettes on my clothes had faded enough at least for that. "How are you feeling?"

He shrugged his answer and dropped off his brief-case in the living room, next to the couch. I followed him into the kitchen and took a seat at the table, while he gave my mom a peck and glanced at the pot on the stove. "Macaroni and cheese, eh?" he said with a grimace. "What am I having?" Dad had stopped eating cheese in bulk a few years before, when he had a cholesterol scare. That's also when he had to have bypass surgery for arteriosclerosis and the doctors warned him about his temper—stress of any kind, even. Luckily, it was right around when Suzanne moved out and went to college, taking most of the reasons he had for losing his temper along with her. Lately he'd been having a lot of stomach pain, too. The doctors were calling it gallstones.

"Halibut." As she answered, she popped open the microwave and pulled out a dish. The stench of fish and lemon hit me in the nose. Awful.

"Just for the halibut," my dad said and smiled at me. Hilarious. So that's where I get it from. Right.

Pretty much since the beginning of time, we've had the same seats at the dinner table. Suzanne and I sat clos-est to the wall, across from each other, Dad sat on my right, and my mom sat across from him. With Suzanne out of the house, across from me was an empty chair, usu-ally used as a spot to store old newspapers. Perfect.

Both my parents have this very dark, very curly hair. They both usually wear glasses, too. When I was much younger, seriously for years, I had no idea there was any difference between "husband and wife" and "brother and sister."

"How was school?" My dad is a psychologist, so he can't talk much about work at dinner.

I shrugged and chewed and swallowed quickly. "Good."

"Anything new?"

"Not really."

"Have you thought about going out for track again this winter?" I used to be a very good runner—the short races, like the 100- and 200-yard runs. That 200-yard race was perfect for me, the coach used to tell me. He thought my running style made the 100 a little too short to use my kick, and the 400 a little too long for my patience. I tend to think he was right.

"I don't know. I might." I didn't want to bring up how much smoking had made it hard to run even the 200. "I don't really like it that much. It's boring. All you do is run. I don't know. . . . What's the point?"

"You used to like it." He was right. I used to love it. I especially loved it when people started calling me Flying Fisher on the junior high team. That's what they used to call my dad when he ran track in high school. Our last name is Fisher.

"I don't know. I'll think about it. I'd have to try out pretty soon." I was really shoveling it now.

"Oh, come on," my mom said, as though she'd heard just about enough. Sometimes my dad sort of sees where she's going and makes this little move with his hand to calm her down. It's weird, because just a couple of years ago someone should have been calming him down. Like I said, he fought with Suzanne all the time—never with me, though. Just with Suzanne, probably because she was always ready to explode herself. He turned a little in his chair to face me. "Simon, you know Mr. Freeman would let you back on the team without a tryout." No doubt about it, actually. He invited me once a week. I just shrugged in reply.

"Well, we're not going to force you to do anything." He went back to his fish. "I don't want to harp on this, but let me say one more thing." Here it comes. "If you join track again, I know you'll be able to stop smoking."

"That's why I can't join." I put down my fork, right into defensive mode.

"What, you don't want to quit now?" My mom dropped her fork, too, only hers landed right in her bowl and flung a macaroni elbow onto her pants. "Shit!"

"No, that's not what I mean." Man, I could whine sometimes. "I mean Freeman's not going to let me stay on the team when he sees I can't run fifty feet without stopping to catch my breath."

My dad placed his fork face down on the plate. He'd finished eating already and was nursing his seltzer. "When did you start smoking, Simon?" It's weird; neither of them had ever asked me that before.

"I don't know. About a year ago." Actually, three years ago. I know the exact date, time, moment, everything. It was just before my thirteenth birthday, with Lily and these two gay guys from the track team. I only did it so I could get used to smoking. I really wanted to start getting high. I only thought of cigarettes as practice.

"Do you really have that much trouble with short-ness of breath already?" He was getting pretty concerned. Amazing thing about my dad: everyone around can be getting emotional and stupid and loud as much as you like, but if he turns to you and talks quiet and smooth and rational, you can't help seeing things his way. It's sort of frightening.

"I don't know. I guess I do a little bit, yeah."

"Well, it's time for you to quit, regardless." My mom was dabbing her pants with a seltzer-soaked napkin, but the little spot of butter and cheese-oil on her thigh wasn't budging. "It's hard, but when I quit, I did it in one try. Just up and quit the moment I learned I was pregnant with Suzanne." Dad took a long swig of his seltzer as she spoke.

"I'll try."

My dad put his hand on my shoulder. He always did that before his closing line. I wondered if at a session he would get up and put his hand on his patient's shoulder when time was up. "Think about track, too. If you could get started with it at all it would help you quit. Pretty soon, you're breathing will be back to normal again. Really."

"I will."

Dad wasn't always so calm and collected. When Suzanne was living at home, he was more Hyde than Jekyll. Their first big fight happened before I was even born, according to my mom. I couldn't imagine what a grown man could have an argument with a four-year-old about. I asked my mom.

She shut her eyes and shrugged as she got up off the living room couch and wandered into the kitchen. I followed behind, and she muttered, "Same thing it's been about every day since, Simon: control."

Maybe it has always been about control. But as Suzanne got older, I guess the fights felt like they were about real things, at least when I can remember them.

I was ten, sitting on the floor of the bathroom closet, surrounded by the smell of towels and gift soaps and Bounce. It was the weekend, and everyone else was home, downstairs, gathered in the official first-round fight room, right there with TV. Someone would turn it off once the volume shot up between Dad and Suzanne. Who wanted smirking, topless men with five-blade razors or glistening, soapy women selling fruit-scented shampoos to witness our family dysfunction?

Mom would be sitting on the couch with her legs and arms crossed, her chin down, wondering when it all went so wrong. But since the TV had clicked off and Suzanne was shrieking already, I knew she and Dad would be on their feet, standing across the coffee table from each other, mouths open or teeth clenched. This time, Mom had found a baggy of weed in Suzanne's jeans pocket.

"Just apologize," I muttered to myself. A little light seeped in under the closet door and I picked at the corner of an old towel at my side. It had that almost-crisp feel that towels get once they've been relegated to beach and picnic use. "Say you won't do it again."

She didn't, though. Principled to the last, I guess. "It's harmless! It's much safer than smoking *cigarettes*!" she shouted. "I don't know a single person who doesn't smoke pot sometimes. Besides, why is *she* going through my jeans?!"

"It's illegal!" Dad shouted over the word "jeans" with a bang: his fist on the veneered entertainment center. "And it's forbidden in this house or anywhere else! Will it be harmless when you end up in court or in jail, or Mom or I end up in jail because of your behavior?!"

The shouting went on. It was up to me to end round one, I knew. Otherwise it ended when Suzanne banged open the front door and went God knew where. I wiped my eyes and took a deep breath, then reached up for the doorknob and opened the closet enough to stick my head out.

"Shut up!"

The screaming stopped. Mom's voice bubbled up, but I couldn't hear what she said. I got up and left the closet and the bathroom. I crossed the gray carpeting in the upstairs hallway and went into my room, crawled into bed.

The silence couldn't last. Dad calmed down. I heard the hum of his voice through the floor, but what he was saying wouldn't have changed. And Suzanne replied, admitting no wrongdoing, never apologizing. "It doesn't have to be sincere, Suzie," I whispered under my covers. "It's just the price of peace. Say it."

Still, the volume went up slowly, until finally Suzanne's voice was too loud, and her words too rebellious, for Dad to listen anymore. His fist struck the furniture again. "Enough!"

Round two would start soon, upstairs. I heard Suzie's feet on the steps and turned so I wouldn't be facing the door when she came in to make sure I knew this was all Dad's fault.

The rest of dinner was easier. I'd aced a recent math test, which was good news to lay on them, and, even though I was struggling through chemistry, we all knew it was my last science class so, as long as I was passing, it wasn't a problem at all. Mom and Dad spent the next hour or so talking about a few movies and shows they wanted to see, and I mainly sat there and listened or let my mind wander.

Dinner used to be different in my house, when Suzanne was still there and when Dad was still working nights. We'd start dinner by five and finish by five-fifteen. It was a bit of a joke. By five-thirty the dishwasher was running, Suzanne was out of the house, Dad was on his way to the office again, and I was killing time in my room or watching TV. Mom would be upstairs watching the Movie of the Week or something.

But Dad stopped working nights when the pains in his stomach started, and he didn't even go in to the office every day, either. After dinner we'd sometimes watch a movie together or play Trivial Pursuit. It used to be only a Friday night thing, when my dad always took the night off. We'd all go out to dinner that night, and Suzanne and I would beg for ice cream on the way home. Well, I'd beg, anyway; I guess Suzanne was sort of pulling my leg, but I didn't care much. Then when we got home, and Suzanne would head out for the night, Dad and I would hang out.

It was pretty cool having him home every night, I guess, especially since I wasn't around much on Fridays anymore. We hung out a lot more. That is, we'd hang out if I didn't fall asleep, and that night, that's exactly what I did. Right after dinner I covered myself completely with my blanket, and grabbed my pillow—hugged it to my chest. And I fell asleep, thinking about Suzanne, and how slowly the light was fading outside, and my grandpa, and my father, and my mom, and the girl at the Gap, and her eyes.

I woke up when everything was quiet and couldn't believe my parents had let me sleep. (They typically wake me up to tell me I'll never sleep through the night if I go to bed that early.) My clock said 4:27, with boxy red numbers hovering near my head. I'd almost made it—two more hours and I'd be up right on schedule. For a few minutes I tried to focus on a star on the ceiling, but they were too dim. They only store a little light I guess, before they die out. That's what I remember thinking before I fell into sleep again. It seemed like seconds had passed when that horrible beeping woke me up, first in the house. I showered and ate quickly and walked to school. I liked to get out before anyone else got up.

| chapter 3 |

My friend Noah joined me for the walk to school, like he did most days since he'd moved into town from California three years before. Since then I'd convinced him to stop wearing those tight jeans—he looked like a total moron. I don't know why I hang out with him, really. I mean, I was a little surprised when I got invited to his bar mitzvah. I'd only known him for about ten minutes; we were partners on some project in physical sciences class. Anyway he's a major pain in the ass—usually has pretty good weed, though.

"What's up, Simon!" Noah always seems more awake than any kid has a right to be. He's also very big on high fives and shit like that. He raised his hand in a pathetic "gimme five" plea, and I offered mine up to receive, sort of casually. Jeez.

The walk to school isn't long. It's through the path, past the strip mall, and across 25A. Noah and I parted ways out front—first period, he's got Spanish on one end and I have English on the other end.

I liked English. The teacher, Mr. Rohan, was a pretty good guy. He was sort of short, with a beard, and he moved around when he lectured—really jumped and hollered. I'm pretty sure he liked me, ever since the first week when I read all of *Our Town* in one night. Major accomplishment. To tell you the truth, it wasn't even that good. I pissed him off quite a bit, though. I don't think he liked that I got high in the morning sometimes. Guarantee, that guy got high in the morning when he was in high school.

Some of the kids said Rohan drank a lot, too. Some kids also said he's gay. I don't know. When he read the first part from *Billy Budd*, I could see why someone would think so—the whole bit about "handsome sailor" and "bronzed mariners." He got very into it.

Rohan was also my adviser for my independent study project, which I had that afternoon. The school has this independent study thing for kids who want to do something that there isn't a class for—in my case, write a lot. There's a creative writing course that's required for freshmen, but it's a total joke and only one semester long. So I decided to get some credit for the writing I was doing anyway. Rohan tried to get me to submit some to the student journal, but I didn't think any of it was worth submitting.

Meanwhile he's the fucking faculty adviser for the thing, so of course he's all rah-rah for it.

"Simon, you'll never know how your work affects a reader if no one ever reads it." He was always saying that.

"I guess it doesn't matter to me how it affects people." And I'd always say that. "I write for me."

There was this one time we met, in October. He sighed loudly and flipped through the latest pages I'd given him. Someone get this guy a drink. "Okay, okay." He pulled out a page and ran his finger down the middle, to about half way. "Right here," he said, leaning over a bit. He smelled like sweat and pipe tobacco. It reminded me of something. "What are you getting at?"

I skimmed the line briefly and shrugged. "I don't know," I grunted, picking at my fingernails. "I just wrote it 'cause I thought it at the time. It's what do you call it. . . ."

"Stream of consciousness." He sighed again and glanced at the clock. Almost four, and then I'm done. "You're not James Joyce, Simon."

I don't even know what he's talking about half the time. "I know."

"Look, all I mean is this style of writing is great for *you*. I know it feels good to let that pour out of your pen. It's like a mental ink explosion." He flipped through the pages some more. "But all a reader sees is the stain it leaves on the page. Until you develop a sense of writing poetically, this won't touch anyone. Maybe a dadaist, but . . ." Again, no idea what he's talking about. He just about cracked himself up, though, I think.

"The piece you gave me last week worked well." That was this thing I'd written about Suzanne and me and the backyard. "I could sense that you'd put some thought into it, rather than rambling on like you sometimes tend to do." Actually, I'd rambled on completely. Truth is, sometimes it comes out right, sometimes it doesn't.

"I thought that one was boring, actually. There's no . . ." I don't know. I was thinking of "fire" or "emotion." They both sounded like bullshit, so I shut up.

"Well, Simon," again with that sigh, "we have to wrap up now. Think about what I said, and please, think about submitting this one to the journal, okay?" He shook the story about Suzanne in my face and got up.

"Okay." I grabbed my bag and my notebook and left the English study hall. I dodged Mr. Freeman near the gym, then found Noah and Lily hanging around out front. Lily's this girl in my grade. I've known her for a few years, and she's sort of on the ugly side. Tremendous tits, though. Noah talks about them often.

"Hey," I said as I stepped outside. The afternoon sun was unbearable. I squinted at the sky, and then at Lily and Noah. "When the hell do we turn the clocks back? I hate all this sun."

"Hi, Simon," said Lily, sort of hopping to my side. She took my arm. "Next week, I think. Sunday, right?"

I shrugged and shook her off my arm so I could pull a cigarette out of my bag. "Can I bum one?"

"Goddamn, Lily, do you ever have your own?" I thrust a butt into my mouth and pulled out another for Lily. Noah, I noticed, was very quietly taking a cigarette from his own pocket.

"Well, *sorry*," you know, with that major accent on the "sorry." Very offended. That's Lily—fucking drama queen. "No one will sell them to me. I don't look old enough." She took the cigarette anyway, of course, and I lit it for her.

"That's because you're not old enough." Rohan had stepped up behind us.

"Oh, Christ," said Noah. I hate it when he says that.

Rohan grabbed the cigarettes from our mouths and stepped them out on the pavement. His face was red. "If I ever catch you on school grounds smoking these fucking things again I will drag you all by the collars right to a long meeting with me, Ms. Gilliard, and your parents."

Shit he was pissed. Lily sort of cowered behind me, like some damsel in distress. Very cute. Noah scanned the pavement, his eyebrows up in a bored sort of face, and I tried to look anywhere but Rohan's eyes. Truth is, I thought I might cry if I did. He just stood there though, and I finally looked up for a second. My eyes got a little wet, but I held it long enough and looked away. He sighed.

"Dammit, Simon. And you, too, Lily." He pulled off his glasses and cleaned the lenses on his shirt sleeve. "The three of you, get out of here." He watched us walk down the path along the side of the school toward the street, and then he headed to his car. When we got around the corner Noah took out another cigarette.

"Fucking prick," he said through closed teeth. He lit the cigarette and then pulled it out of his mouth. "Shit!"

"Keep it down, man," I said. He gets very excited pretty easily. Lily had my arm again, and the three of us started walking over to the mall. "He's not a prick, anyway."

"Yeah he is, and he's gonna have my dad all over me, too." Noah's dad is a *major* fucking prick. Hits him a lot, calls him a fag all the time. Real class act. He's a doctor, into stocks and bonds and shit. Major hotshot.

"Don't sweat it. He won't do anything." I shook off Lily again, who started babbling about her French class. I interrupted her. "Look, if you guys are going to just hang around at the mall, I'm going home." I knew Lily would want to roam around the Gap for a while, and I wasn't up for it. Noah had to open his mouth.

"I'm thinking of going over to the Gap." He was sort of bouncing on his feet. He dropped his cigarette and twisted it out with his foot for like an hour. "I'm gonna hook up with this girl who works there."

I glared at him and said, "Who?" The girl's dark eyes flashed in my head for an instant. Lily stepped back a little and pretended not to listen. Meanwhile I was remembering beating off the day before and was pretty interested in getting home.

"I don't know her *name*," said Noah, like I'd asked an incredibly stupid question. "She's got beautiful tits."

"You're not hooking up with anyone." I smirked at him. Lily looked over at me and squinted.

"Shut up." Noah gets very dense around girls—good-looking ones, anyway. I do too, but I figure I'm at least smart enough to keep my mouth shut. "Want to get some CDs?" It never took much convincing to get Noah to change his plans. Lily looked at me again.

"No, I'm not allowed in there anymore." I'd been caught trying to walk out with a few CDs a couple of months before. Don't get the wrong idea. I'm not some klepto. I just sometimes take shit for laughs. "I'm just going home. I'll see you guys later."

I walked through the parking lot, right past the Gap. She might have been in there, but I didn't see her. When I reached the path, I turned around and saw Noah stepping on and off the curb in front of the record store, waving his arms around and probably rambling on about something, and Lily sitting at his feet, looking at the ground.

| chapter 4 |

I opened the front door and heard my dad coughing in the living room and my mom laughing into the phone. She has a phone laugh. It's a real laugh, but she projects it better when she's on the phone, I guess so the other person knows for sure that whatever they said was positively hilarious. "Hey, Dad." He was in the living room, reading the *Times*. He was wearing jeans and a Yankee shirt. "No work today, huh?"

"Hey, kid," he said, and smiled. He folded up the paper slowly—looked like he was finishing up a sentence. You know, the news—highly absorbing stuff. Then he looked up at me. He looked a little tired. "Meet with Mr. Rohan today?" I leaned in for a quick hug.

"Yeah." I sat down on the couch and looked out the window into our backyard. My mind wandered as I watched a squirrel hop the fence at the far end. Suzanne and I used to go over the fence in our backyard. There, about twenty yards out, was a drop, a steep grassy slope that led right down to the expressway. From the living room it looked like woods, deep and dense, but when you got right in there you could see the drop, and I'll never forget the first time Suzanne lifted me over the fence and walked me to the edge. I must have been very young—seven or eight.

We stood there, just a few feet from sliding down to the expressway. There was so much traffic on that summer Sunday afternoon. It made me smile. Huge, authoritative trucks boomed along. The cars looked tiny compared to them, swerving around them or desperately sliding out from between two. It was so comforting in a way. That was peace. Maybe there's nothing more peaceful than looking down on havoc.

Most times we went over that fence it was for a few minutes when Mom and Dad's backs were turned. Suzanne would hide beer there when she was in high school. I never told anyone about that, even though I hated that she did it. In a way I guess I was proud she'd told me about it, too.

The last time we went was just before Suzanne went to college. I got over the fence on my own and sat on the edge, watching the traffic. It was hardly moving at all. Suzanne sat down next to me. I didn't even look at her. "I think you suck."

"I suck?" she said back to me. "Trust me, when it's time for you to leave, you'll be as excited as I am about it."

"Great. That's not for like over five years." I pulled at the grass in front of me and watched the dark soil crumble off the roots and onto my white socks. "How am I supposed to survive without you around for that long?" I remember looking up at her, and the sun catching my eye. Her browning hair looked all red again, and a tear developed in the corner of my eye. She took my hand, and I turned away.

"Sun's in your eye?" she said, and I could sense her little eyebrow trick. I flipped her the finger, and she laughed and dropped my hand. "You'll be fine," she said, getting to her feet. "Believe me, it'll be a breeze without me around."

My dad cleared his throat a few times and brought me back to the living room. Right, we were talking about Rohan. "Um, he said I should submit one of my stories to the journal."

"You should." He was absolutely beaming.

I changed the subject. "Who's she talking to?" I forgot that it bothered my dad when I called my mom "she." I don't know what he expected me to use if not "she."

"Your aunt Jo." She's always talking to her younger sister. They must have five conversations a day, some three hours long, some three seconds. We heard the sound of the phone being hung up. "Our son is a famous writer!" Dad called out. He looked at me and laughed.

"Come on," I squeaked, and I got up. "I'm going upstairs."

"I'm only kidding." My dad grabbed my arm to stop me. "Don't be so sensitive." His favorite thing to say. That or "self-defeatist." Whenever I'd screw up in school, I was being "self-defeatist," couldn't be that I just screwed up. Had to be some subconscious crap. Comes with having a shrink for a dad.

I plopped back down on the couch as my mom came in for the scoop. Thank God the phone rang. The phone can't ring more than one and a half times before my mom grabs it. My dad and I almost never answer the phone. "Horrible invention," my dad said with a smile.

I could hear my mom's voice from the kitchen. It was Suzanne. I hopped up and picked up the extension in the den. "Hi, Simon. How's everything?"

"Okay."

"I'll let you two talk a little," said my mom, and the phone clicked.

"Just okay?"

"Yeah, I guess. How's school?"

"Eh, you know—class, beer, all that. Nothing too exciting. You dating any girls I should know about?"

"No." I thought about telling her about the girl at the Gap, or even about Lily. There was a long pause. I couldn't say anything.

I only visited my sister at school in Boston one time. I was thirteen, almost fourteen, and some of my parents' friends were going up that way, so I got a ride with them. I couldn't help feeling guilty as I saw her standing out in front of her dorm, waiting for me. We'd barely been in touch at all. It was her fault as much as mine I guess.

"Hi!" She was genuinely glad to see me. I had no idea she was missing me too, but I guess she was. I watched my parents' friends drive off and walked coolly over to Suzanne. She rolled her eyes at me and picked me up with a groan. "My god, what do you weigh now?"

I glared at her. "All right, all right," I said. I couldn't help smiling a little bit, though. It wasn't every day that someone was that glad to see me. I returned her hug, and she took my hand and led me to her room. I thought about pulling away my hand when a few of her friends walked by, but I couldn't bring myself to do it.

"This is my little brother." It's how she introduced me to everyone that weekend. Sometimes she'd mention my name, sometimes not. Sometimes she'd add, "Don't we look alike?" A few of her friends said I was cuter, and I blushed. I just wanted to get to Suzanne's room and sit there with her—just watch her like I did when I was young.

Even though she tossed me a "So, what's up?" and cocked her eyebrows, she did most of the talking, and it was perfect. She got us a pizza and let me talk for a few minutes about what teachers I had. Then she just went off. She remembered out loud about when she was thirteen, and she told me stories about myself that made me blush again. She talked about Mom and Dad in a way I never thought she would—like she really loved them both. It seemed off, but definitely honest, and—it was something in her voice—I sort of got choked up. She stopped for a moment then and looked like she was too, but she managed to get me smiling again as her roommate came in:

"This is Simon, my little brother. Don't we look alike?" She bounded over to me and sat down at my side, pushing her face up against mine. My hair was still redder, and my freckles were darker, but it was true. We did still look alike.

"A little, but he's cuter."

Suzanne laughed. "I know, I know," and she gave me a peck on the cheek.

The next day, Suzanne woke me up. I'd slept in her roommate's bed. I guess her roommate had a serious boyfriend she stayed with, so her bed was usually empty at night. "Are you ready to do Boston, kid?" Without lifting the blanket from my head, I could picture Suzanne sitting beside me, probably dressed and doing up her sneakers. I groaned.

"Can we eat breakfast?" The light through the blinds struck me as I pulled away the blanket, but I smiled when I saw her eyes looking down at me—hazel. She looked beautiful; the sun gave her hair a shimmering halo.

"Of course," she said, getting up and grabbing her Yankee hat. "I know somewhere we could even get a half-decent bagel."

"Okay," I said, swinging my legs around and sitting up. "You still wear that hat, huh?" It was the same Yankee hat she'd been wearing for years, and for a hundred years before that my father wore it. It was faded and ragged, and the strap in the back was taped up and sticky.

"Of course I do," she said with a cock of her head. "Gotta represent."

"Word."

"You drink coffee yet?"

I shrugged and yawned. "Sure." I didn't, though—not then. Not without whipped cream and chocolate sauce and various suffixes like "-lattafrappaccino," anyway.

Suzanne took me on a walking tour of Boston that morning. I added about a gallon of milk and enough sugar to bake an angel food cake to my coffee and nursed it as we walked. Boston is a nice city, but the bagels are *not* half-decent, and most of what she showed me was a bit too much like history class.

"I prefer New York," I said when we got back to her place. I smirked and felt for a moment like New York. I felt dark and gritty, and burnt like coffee long after break-fast—a deeper sort of cool. It made me want a cigarette. "Do you have any cigarettes?"

She shot me the "loser" eyebrows, and I laughed a little. So much for cool. Suzanne, you have no idea what a fucking loser I am.

"Hello?"

Suzanne's voice crackled through the cordless phone, and I shook. I suddenly felt pretty down. I hate talking on the phone, even to Suzanne. I just hate it. I can't see her, I can't see her eyes, and I can't touch her.

"There's really nothing going on."

"All right, whatever." She sighed a bit—sounded let down. It was just how I felt. "Stop smoking, Simon, okay? Really."

"Oh, come on, Suzanne. Don't do that." That was low. Way to make me feel even more like shit, sis. "I'll put Mom back on."

I handed over the cordless to my mom and went up to my room. I wasn't planning on it, but I beat off anyway. I just wanted to stop thinking about Suzanne for a few minutes, and smoking. I tried thinking about this freshman girl who's really cute, but that didn't work—felt horrible—so I went back to the girl at the Gap. Then I fell asleep. The worst kind of sleep: as soon as I was falling my mom knocked at the door and shouted something about dinner.

Dinner that night was fucking tragic—just my dad going on and on. Suzanne says I sound depressed, I really have to stop smoking, blah blah. Then my mom went on about the socks I'd stolen the day before. I don't know how the hell she knew; must have found the receipt or something I guess. It's a major deal—a pair of socks from the Gap. I apologized my ass off and ate quickly. We had steak. I always had mine very well-done, as close to leather as it could get without bursting into flames. I hate the way the pink part in the middle feels like flesh in my mouth. Makes me want to throw up.

When I finally got paroled from the dinner table I hurried upstairs and closed the door. I grabbed my copy of *Billy Budd* and started reading. Man, could that guy go on. After a few pages I had to put it down and pick up *The Sun Also Rises* instead. I love that book. I read for an hour or so and then took a few hits by the window. Then I started writing.

OCTOBER 30

... there's no heaven there's no hell. dark suits crowded through the door and drifted to the long tables. beneath vinyl-coated white cloths they were pressed sawdust and sweepings held together by glue and snot and the aluminum band to give them shape. after the funeral they'd be wiped down. the cloths would come off. the tables would be folded up, leaned against a wall in a basement with a cement floor. my aunt is having lox. my cousins are darting across the lawn, dodging each other in the parking lot. grandpa's worm food. . . .

| chapter 5 |

I meet with Rohan twice a week for my independent study. I always have something for him to read, but it's usually the messy stuff he wants me to avoid. I once brought him this ten page thing I'd done, about my grandpa's death and funeral. It was pretty funny, I think.

"You have an interesting sense of humor, Simon." Rohan was leering at me, with his head down and his eyes up, looking over his glasses. He's a very weird guy. He looked back at the page, flipped through a little, and looked back at me. "'There's no heaven, there's no hell. . . . Grandpa's worm food'?" He dropped the paper on the table and looked at me. Then he leaned back and crossed his arms.

What? He let out a big sigh. "It's that simple, eh, Simon?" I turned my head and shrugged a little. "Hm?"

"Yeah, I guess it is." Gimme a break.

"When your grandpa died, this is how you felt?" He leaned in for a second. "This is about your grandfather, isn't it?" I nodded. "And this was your take on the situation?"

I shrugged again and glanced at the clock. Three thirty. Great. "I was only joking around. Look, what else do you want me to say? We're atheists. There's nothing else to it." I grabbed the story off the table and started putting it away. "Forget it then."

"Don't take me the wrong way, Simon." He looked a little worried then. "I'm glad you're writing in a more concrete style. But I think you have a much more mature take on this that you're just not tapping." He picked up his red pen and flipped it in his hand. "I want you to go deeper."

What is this, therapy? Honestly, I don't think it gets much deeper. It might look like some tepid black comedy at first glance, but that's the whole point. I was raised without God, so there are no deeper answers. After my grandpa died, my dad asked me if I knew what was happening. I said, "Sure." But neither of us was really sure. My dad thought he was sure, until the very end, but that's nonsense. My grandma is fucking ancient now, and even she, a born-and-raised communist-atheist-Russian Jew, believes in her heart that Grandpa is waiting for her on the other side.

I hate being atheist, but I can't seem to shake it. I suppose it only bothers me because everyone else I know was bar mitzvahed in junior high. Ever since then I've been on the outside. Even Lily and Noah did Hebrew school. Or maybe it is deeper than that. Maybe I want those answers just like everyone else.

My grandpa died in the winter when I was twelve, in seventh grade. That was a banner fucking year. My mother told me he'd died before I left for school that morning, and I didn't feel a thing. It wasn't until fifth period, history class, that I was struck, and I had to get up and go to the bathroom to cry. After that, I didn't cry much again until the service. There were so many people there, and whenever anyone would smile I'd break down. I'd get so angry. There shouldn't have been any smiling in that room.

I don't remember how soon after the service it was. I was sitting on the top step in my house, watching my father. He was only getting ready for work I suppose, shaving maybe, or doing his tie. Suddenly I had to hold him, and though he must have thought I was upset over grandpa, I was more upset over him—over my father. I've only felt pity for my father twice in my life, and that was the first time. He'd lost his father. I imagined the pain, and I never wanted to know it firsthand.

"I'm going to give you a book." I had completely forgotten where I was. Rohan had gotten up and walked into his office. He came out with a thin black book. "It's called *Endgame*, by Samuel Beckett, an Irish playwright who wrote in French. I think you'll find it interesting."

"I don't read French," I replied without picking up the book.

Rohan dropped it into my lap. "This is the English version, Simon," he said.

"Okay." I picked up the book and glanced at the cover, then slipped it into my bag.

"Don't bring me any writing next week. Just read that." He tapped the table top with his forefinger, hard enough that his finger sort of bent back. Angry little man. Then he got up and grabbed his satchel.

"It won't take more than hour or so," he said as he started walking off. "We'll talk about it." I watched him go into his office and close the door, and for a few minutes I just sat there, getting back into my thoughts. I watched the hallway from my seat. It was nearly four, so not much was going on. A couple of black kids walked by, in a hurry, probably on the way to football practice. I didn't know their names. There are only about twenty black kids in the whole school, and they pretty much keep to themselves. There's even an alcove, on the other side of the gym, where they all hang out between periods, or when they don't go to class. Freshmen are told not to go over there, even though it's a great shortcut from the front of the building to the English wing. I did once and got punched real hard in the back. A bunch of guys laughed at me, and then the guy that had hit me mussed my hair and said I was all right.

I read *Endgame*, by the way. I told Rohan it all seemed pretty pointless to me—made running circles around a track seem fucking productive.

| chapter 6 |

My dad went in for surgery on a Friday in November, to
have his gallbladder removed. My mother had had the
same surgery like twenty years before or something—I
mean, like not exactly modern medicine compared with
today—so I wasn't thinking it was any sort of big deal. My
mom went with him to the hospital, and I went to school.
I walked with Noah and we saw Lily out front. The three
of us went to smoke a little before first period. Actually, I
got pretty high, higher than I meant to, and decided not
to go to Rohan's class. I didn't tell Noah or Lily that my
dad was in the hospital.

"What happened to your eye, Noah?" Lily asked.
Noah had a black eye again. I knew what it was from.

"Dad popped me good last night." He passed the
bowl to Lily and took out a cigarette. He's always lighting

cigarettes between hits. What a waste. "I don't even care."
I mumbled what a prick the guy is and lay back.

Lily started playing with my hair. "Do you guys want
to go to this party tomorrow night?"

Groan, Lily. Sounds fun.

"What party?" Noah lit another cigarette and got to
his feet.

"Kyle Aaronson's parents are away for the week," Lily
said. "He's throwing an open-house on Saturday."

I sat up, mainly so Lily would stop touching my head.

"Sure, I'll go." Noah started doing that bouncing
thing.

The idea of standing in some kid's backyard with a
bunch of assholes sipping shit beer from a plastic cup didn't
exactly thrill me to my toes. I rubbed my eyes and tried to
look at my watch. Couldn't see too straight. "What time
is it? Is it second period yet?"

Lily stood up and checked her watch. "In ten minutes."

I slowly got up. "All right. I'm going in." Noah gave
me a mock salute and laughed. Lily squinted at me and
took a step back and a step forward—making up her mind
to follow me inside or not. Shit, she needed to grow up or
grow a pair—or a clit or some fucking thing. "Coming
with me, Lil?" She shrugged, no big deal. Right.

"Yeah, okay." Lily and I had second period together—
social studies. She came to my side and we walked together.
It was sort of nice; she didn't try to take my arm or anything. I almost told her about my dad, but I didn't want to

mess it up. Lily talked a little, about some other girls in our grade and what bitches they are. It was all right.

It was toward the end of class when there was a knock on the door and some kid stuck his head in. Mr. Hillenbrand had a couple of words with him and went back to the front of the class. "Simon," he announced. Shit. Buzz, killed. "Go down to Ms. Gilliard's office."

"Why?"

"I don't know, Simon," replied Hillenbrand. He picked up his chalk and got ready to continue teaching. I glanced at Lily, and she shrugged at me, so I just left. I picked up my bag and started down the hall to Gilliard's office. I shouldn't have. I should have walked the other way.

When I got there, my aunt Jo—my mom's little sister—was already there, and she looked like shit. She was crying, and when she saw me she just started fucking wailing. She grabbed me and hugged me and cried like crazy. I'm telling you, I just should have walked the other way. Right the hell out of the school, across the street, past my house and on past Boston, past everything, forever.

I couldn't really breathe. The sides of my head started to hurt, and I just stood there while my aunt bawled on my head. She finally started to talk through those crying burps and gasps. I could see Ms. Gilliard out of the corner of my eye, standing there very awkwardly. She wasn't looking at us. "Simon." My aunt kept croaking my name. "It looks like Daddy has cancer." I bit down hard, until my temples started to hurt, and then I clenched my fists until my nails dug into my palms, and then it wasn't enough, so I pulled away from her and kicked the chair by the wall. It fucking hurt, too, but the chair flipped and knocked into the wall. Ms. Gilliard moved toward me a little but stepped back again quickly. I guess she did the math in her head quickly: student damages chair divided by father with cancer equals leave it alone.

I know, by the way. I had a pretty over-the-top reaction. People survive cancer all the time now, but I wasn't seeing it that way. I mean, every old person I know has survived cancer already. But everyone eventually dies of cancer too.

I looked up at Jo. "Are we going over to the hospital? Is Mom over there?"

My aunt nodded.

"Is your car out front? In the circle?"

She nodded again, and I left the office and ran to the front of the school. I just tore down the hall, my fists tights, my teeth clenched, until I reached the car, and I stood there, catching my breath, waiting for my aunt to catch up, thinking about having a cigarette, and wondering if anyone had called Suzanne. I decided not to smoke; I didn't want to calm down. So I screamed instead. I heard my aunt's footsteps coming down the halls. She must have heard me scream, because she was running.

The ride to the hospital was pretty rough. Jo seemed to have gained a little control of herself, I guess since she had to concentrate on driving. She didn't say a word, and

I certainly didn't. She only occasionally put her hand on my arm or something. Every time she did I had to clench my teeth. When she wasn't touching me I thought I might fall asleep.

I won't get into gory details. In a nutshell, they went in, found cancer all over the place near the gallbladder, and closed him up again. My mom was a wreck. She was sort of camped out in an intern's office next to the OR waiting room. He was being pretty decent, giving her coffee and letting her use the phone and all. Once we got there I had to sit with my mom, holding her, for quite a while. Jo started making calls. I heard her call Suzanne. She started bawling again as she told her what was going on.

Meanwhile, my dad was being taken up to a room upstairs for recovery. That night was the worst. My mom and Jo and I went up to the room and sat with him while he fell in and out of sleep. Jo took me home, and Mom stayed in the room with Dad overnight. I went inside my house. It was empty and dark. There were a bunch of messages on the machine, but I didn't check them. I just went into the living room and sat on the couch by the window, where I could hear the traffic flying by on the expressway out back. And then I cried. I cried until I fell asleep where I was.

That night I dreamed about my sister. She was crying and moaning and the tears ran down her face like rust. I tried to hold her, but her body collapsed in my arms like an empty duffel bag. I looked down at her eyes and they were black and wet and huge. She wouldn't close her mouth—just kept bawling. I tried to stifle her, but I couldn't, so I dropped her, limp, onto the rug in the den. She looked up at me, now silent, and I felt my eyes growing swollen and wet. The phone finally woke me up, and I felt complete relief. The dream washed away when sunlight came in through the window over my head, and I rolled over to answer the phone. It was Jo.

The minute I heard her voice, images from the night before struck me, and the dread I'd felt while I slept came back times ten, times a hundred. I couldn't bear it, I guess, because after she said she'd come by to pick me up, I hung up the phone and really started freaking out. The crying started again, and I found myself on the floor, rolling and wailing like I'd been shot. I tried to get into the drama of it; that helped calm me down. I imagined I was the main character in a movie, and I got very stoic and cool. I started pacing and mumbling to myself. The phone rang again.

"Hi, Simon." Suzanne.

"Hi."

"How are you doing?"

I didn't answer for a while. I didn't want to say it. "Fine."

"Really?" She didn't believe me. No kidding.

"No. I'm not doing so good." I started choking a little.

"Shit. Is Jo coming to get you?"

I nodded into the phone. "Uh-huh."

"Okay. I'm getting on a flight now. I'm coming into LaGuardia at eleven-forty."

"Good." God, I couldn't even talk. I felt like such a kid.

"Simon, write it down." I moved into the kitchen and took a pen and a slip of paper off the message pad. My hand was shaking and stiff, but I managed to get it down.

"What's the flight number?" I heard my own voice. It was jumbled and tinny, and I couldn't focus on the paper anymore. The doorbell rang.

Suzanne heard it through the phone. "Is that Jo?" I opened the door and gave Jo the phone. Then I went and sat down by the window again, listening to the express-way. A car braked hard and skidded and I shook, waiting for the crash. It never came.

Jo came in and took my hand and led me to the car. She took my keys and locked the door behind us. The drive was pretty much the same, except now Jo was pet-ting the back of my head the whole way. It didn't make me stressed this time; it felt right. I didn't speak, or clench my teeth. I just sat, numb. It actually felt good.

Dad was awake when we got there. Mom was even smiling. Jo was the only one acting frazzled. I gave my dad a light hug. "How are you feeling, Dad?" I was crying a little. It sucks seeing your dad like that, looking totally helpless. His glasses were off, he looked more tired than ever, and there were a couple of tubes coming out of his arm. He smiled though.

He shrugged a bit and opened his mouth a little. He looked like he hadn't had anything to eat or drink in a month, and when his lips parted they fought to stay together for a painful few seconds, dry and cracked and ugly, more the pale color of his face than pink. Somehow I could hear him breathe out, "Okay. Nothing hurts right now."

He took hold of my hand and went on about the painkillers they were giving him, trying to be funny. But his voice was so quiet and parched, and in that silent, white room, it reminded me of Marlon Brando in *The Godfather*, when he asked Robert Duval where Al Pacino was. I almost smiled when I remembered the famous scene at the hospital, picturing myself standing out front with my hand in my coat, knowing I was only bluffing—there was no gun in there at all.

"How are you holding up?" He tried to curve his dry lips into a smile. It was one of the worst things I've ever seen.

"I'm okay." Then he knew. I wasn't sure if they'd tell him as soon as he came to, or if they'd wait a little while, and for how long. "I'm fine." Some people were moving around in the room—it might have been Jo, or a nurse. I'm not sure. I couldn't take my eyes off my dad, his own sunken eyes, glasses off. My ears started ringing then, and my dad wasn't looking at me anymore. He was watching the door. His doctor had just come in.

This guy was a real presence. He was big, and his voice boomed. He seemed to find a sense of the room—at first his face was tentative, but then he smiled and shook all our hands. It wasn't any real sort of smile, more like a pleasant resignation. It said, "This sucks, doesn't it? Ain't life funny like that?" The weird part was that I sort of enjoyed it, watching him squirm a little. I thought for a minute about Ms. Gilliard, and how she couldn't watch Jo and me freaking out in her office. She just didn't know how to handle it.

I turned to watch the doctor while he spoke, as my hearing came back into focus, only picking up every few words, things like "chemo" and "surgery" and "options" and "pancreas" and "polyps." My parents got very serious and listened. Jo came to my side and put her arm around my shoulder. That's when the dark started to fade a little.

My dad had a lot of questions, and he seemed to sit up a bit more—he even put his glasses on. I can't really remember anything he said, or any little comments my mom inserted, or how the doctor replied. It wasn't what they said that made me feel positive all of a sudden; it was my dad coming back to himself, speaking with some authority, his voice smoothing out a little and ringing of intelligence, like it would be when he talked politics with his brother or Suzanne. He seemed in charge, like he should.

My mom started writing a bunch of things down. She'd probably seen something on *Oprah* about it—some expert explaining how important it is to take notes when serious medical issues come up. Jo immediately ran over and offered to take notes for her, so my mom wouldn't be troubled I guess. I watched Jo plead for a few minutes. She looked so scared, so helpless and so afraid of being helpless. I sat down in the chair in the corner by the window and listened to the traffic go by. Suzanne would land soon.

NOVEMBER 12

with the shade all the way down
the stars on the ceiling are faded
and it's dark

i'm waiting for the light to come through the door
and up the stairs and into my room
to hold me

| chapter 7 |

"Nobody dies of cancer anymore." Lily and I were sitting on the curb in front of her house. "Stacy's mom got breast cancer like five years ago, and she's totally fine now."

Lily had no idea what she was talking about. I'd googled "pancreatic cancer," and almost everyone who gets it dies.

Lily put her arm around me and rubbed my shoulder. I shook her off and picked up a pebble off the street.

"Don't tell anyone, okay?"

She squinted at me and nodded: *okay*. She looked like she was going to cry for a minute, and then she looked away again. My dad's Camry came rolling slowly up Cardinal Drive. Suzanne was driving. "I gotta go."

"Okay." She got up as I did and took my hand, but I couldn't look at her. I should never have told her. It had been a couple of weeks since my dad's surgery, and he was starting chemotherapy that day. His brother, my uncle Abe, was a heavyweight in hospital administration, so he'd found Dad this doctor in Manhattan—some pioneer type, world famous, loose cannon, bound to achieve greatness, and all that. Apparently he was into being really gung-ho about the whole thing. Just get in there and start killing the stuff. I guess Abe figured this doctor was their best shot up against the worst cancer there is.

Mom and Dad left the house that morning at around seven. That might have been the first time my mom drove into Manhattan since they moved out here to Long Island, with my dad in the passenger seat.

We were about halfway home when Suzanne finally said anything. "Is that your girlfriend?"

"No." I guess I sort of snapped it at her. She looked at me sideways.

"Okay." We turned onto Powerhouse Road, and Suzanne sighed big—real dramatic. I really started hating those resigned sighs, like I was some kind of lost cause. I'd heard them my whole life, and now Suzanne was laying that crap on me.

I clicked on the radio to a station I knew would drive Suzanne a little nuts. Since she's been in college she hasn't liked any normal music at all. She listens to jazz and freaky way-out garbage from India and crap like that. So I put on this hard rock station. This great song came on.

Really heavy, Mudvayne or something. Suzanne would have loved it like two or three years before that. I mean, if it wasn't for her blasting Helmet and Biohazard from her room when she was in high school, I don't think I'd be into this heavy shit at all. Instead she just lowered the volume until I could barely hear it at all.

"Not now, Simon, okay?" She gave me another one of those sighs. God, I'd have given anything for an eyebrow twitch again. "You still listen to stuff like this?"

"What does that mean?" Very offended. I was dying to scream at her all of sudden. She was a complete traitor.

"I don't know," and she half shrugged. "I just think you're smarter than this stuff."

I sat and stewed until we'd pulled up in front of the house. I didn't wait for Suzanne to put the car in park; just hopped out the second we'd stopped and went inside. My parents were both sitting in the living room. Well, my dad was actually reclining and looking real tired.

"Hey, kid." He folded up the paper and dropped it, along with the pen he was using to do the crossword puzzle, on the carpet next to the couch. He didn't look happy; he has this look he gets sometimes, a sort of sad smile. It was the same one I remember him giving me at my grandpa's funeral, and the same one he'd give when I would mope around the house or start crying because I missed Suzanne so much after she'd left for college.

"Where's your sister?" My mom had been on the phone, probably with Jo, but she got off in a hurry when

I came in. I didn't think she was worried about me over-hearing anything. They just wanted to talk to us. And this was obviously going to be some big talk, a major deal.

"Right here," chirped Suzanne as she plopped onto the couch next to my dad. He let out a little "oomph" and gave her a little tap on the knee. "What's up?"

Dad cleared his throat and dropped the sad smile after a glance in my direction. I decided to sit down in the chair farthest from the couch. I clenched my teeth, ready for anything.

"There are some things we ought to talk about," he went on.

"Okay. Shoot," Suzanne piped in. She gets a little chatty when she's nervous, though I don't think most people would notice it. She's usually quite chatty, but this is a different sort. A cuter, younger sort, that makes me feel sorry for her. I suddenly felt very bad about sitting so far from them, but I knew if I moved to the couch just then I'd lose the grip on the arm of the chair, and lose the clench in my teeth, and then I might just lose control completely.

"We have to talk about what will happen if I die." Everyone looked at me. Dad put his hand on Suzanne's knee and looked at me. Mom put her hand on her mouth and looked at me. And Suzanne bit her lip and looked at me. I just clenched my teeth harder and watched my dad as he went on. He told us how expensive it was to bury his father, and Mom told us about a woman she worked with who struggles every week, still paying for the funeral she gave her husband. And she's nearly seventy.

"Your mom and I have talked about this before, and I'd like as little as possible to be spent on services. I don't want a proper funeral. No burial. It makes far more sense to choose cremation. Is that okay with both of you?"

He was really asking, as if I'll give a shit about this when my dad is dead. So I nodded my head quickly and clenched harder. It was getting harder to sit alone and to maintain my grip. I wished to God that Suzanne would rush to me to hold me up. She didn't. "Of course," she said, and took Dad's hand.

"I don't want any Jewish association at all. No grave-side service, and certainly no unveiling." I remembered my grandpa's unveiling and was glad to hear there would be none of that crap. I considered it a sick joke: to grab a kid, a year healthier and happier than he was when his grandpa died, and force him to start mourning all over again practically.

"For you guys," and he glanced at Suzanne and me, "and for Mom, if you want to have a very simple service, I think that would be a good idea." Neither of us reacted. I just lowered my head. I couldn't clench any harder, and I tried like crazy to stop a giant tear from splashing onto my knee. I don't think anyone saw.

He went on. "You don't have to, but services, memorials, funerals . . . they do make it easier for people to start mourning in a healthy way." Psychology. I hate psychology. "People could speak, if they wanted to, to say a few words." "People"—as if it would be some people we didn't know, just some strangers who might decide to show up. Not the three of us who would be left behind.

I got to my feet, but I didn't lift my head. "I don't want to talk about this." I was really crying now. "I really don't want to talk about this." I took a step toward the stairs, then back, always with my eyes on the rug. There was a dingy patch, a path from the hallway through to the TV room.

"You have to," my dad said, sort of stern. To me it felt like a ridiculous time to be stern about a crybaby son. If I ever had the right to be a big crybaby, I think this was the moment. "This is something Mom and I feel you and Suzanne should be involved in."

I shook my head real fast and wiped my eyes on my sleeve. "Fine," I snapped. "Fine. I think it's fine. Whatever you guys want is fine. Okay?" The shaking in my head got my feet going and I started pacing a little in front of my chair. I was itching to leave that room.

Suzanne looked like she might get up for a second, but she only whispered, "Simon," and trailed off.

"Why are we talking about this?" I was starting to scream a little bit. "You—you just started—getting treatment today! Shit!" Those crying-hiccups were jumping out of my throat. Suzanne and my mom and dad just sat there and watched me lose it. "Can't we even give it—give it a chance? I mean—we don't have to talk about this yet! I don't want to talk about this now!" I stopped pacing and waving my arms and put my face in my hands. My shoulders bent and my knees snapped straight and I stood stock still, waiting and crying. Everyone let me wait, and after a few minutes I opened my eyes and stared at my palms, catching my breath.

"Are we done?" I spoke very calmly and I think quietly, and looked up. Suzanne looked at my eyes, and then at my dad.

"I guess so," he said. He looked disappointed. I turned slowly and started to walk out of the room. I was so tired, exhausted. It felt so good. I wanted to sleep.

"Simon." It was my mom. She was getting off the couch, and Suzanne was watching her get up. Everything went so slowly.

"Let him alone," my dad said, and she stopped and pouted at me when I turned around. I glanced at Suzanne, inviting her to follow me out, and then went up to my room. I left the door ajar, hoping she'd stick her head in to check on me. She always used to do that when I was upset. She'd say, "Knock, knock?" and then sit on the edge of my bed and squeeze my foot.

But no one came. I just lay there and eventually fell asleep—didn't even get high. I hadn't smoked any weed at all since the morning my dad went in for surgery. I never planned it that way, never swore off the stuff or anything; it just sort of worked out that way. It helped that I'd been sort of dodging Noah most of the time. I walked to school with him still, but after that I didn't see him all day. Avoided the whole situation.

| chapter 8 |

"Man, I haven't gotten high with you in a while." Noah half squinted at me as we walked to school that Thursday morning. "Where you been?"

I felt my eyes dart in my head, uncomfortably. "I've been around. You know, my sister's still in town, so I've hung out with her a lot." Major bull. Truth is, I'd been loner-ing it. When I did cut class, I'd head down to the highway and sit under the overpass, watching cars go by. They really fly in the middle of the day.

"Is she still in town? Doesn't she have to go back up for classes?" I'd told Noah that Suzanne was down for Thanksgiving. Really, there's no Thanksgiving break that's two weeks long.

"She's going back up tonight for finals week, actually." I spotted Lily waiting for us by the front of the school. She waved. Neither of us waved back.

"Cool! My parents are leaving town tonight. You definitely gotta come over and smoke up, man. My cousin out in San Francisco got me the kindest bud." I zoned as he went on about red hairs and shit like that, and just watched Lily waiting for us. She looked up to check our progress every so often, but mostly kept her eyes in a book. I sometimes forget she's smart as hell. We all do, the three of us. We all forget we're smart as hell.

"Yeah, okay. I'll definitely come by tonight, after Suzanne leaves."

"Nice."

We reached Lily, but I only said "hey" and "later" before walking off quickly to English. I heard Noah ask Lily, "What's up with Simon?" and Lily reply, "Shut up," as the door closed behind me. I was late, and the halls were nearly empty. My sneakers squeaked as I dragged my feet down the main hall and through the shortcut past the gym and into the English wing. Rohan glanced at me and quickly away as I slid into my desk toward the back. He was lecturing about *Winesburg, Ohio*.

"Everything all right, Simon?" he asked, checking my name off on his roster. I knew I was in the "incomplete" high-risk group.

"Yeah, fine." I tried not to sound especially smug.

He looked over his glasses at me, his red pen still hovering over his attendance book. "You're down to four more absences, Simon."

"I know, Mr. Rohan." I spoke as I pulled out my copy of *Winesburg, Ohio* and my notebook.

"You do know that every lateness is one-third of an absence?" He was glancing at the book, counting with the tip of his pen.

"Yes." It was getting harder not to sound smug. I searched for my pen in my green satchel, but only pulled out a twisted, gnarly, leaking mutant. My right hand was stained black. "Aw, fuck."

A few people laughed at me. It wasn't the first time.

"Excuse me, Mr. Fisher?" Rohan rarely pulled that "mister" stuff.

"Can I go wash my hands?"

He never pulled that "I don't know. Can you?" crap either.

The closest bathroom was down at the end of the English wing. My freshman year I went in there one time and found some greaser seniors walloping this guy Robin from track who everyone thought was probably queer. They had dragged him into a stall and were about to flush his head when I walked in.

"Um . . . should I come back another time?" I hadn't meant it to be funny at all. The greasers howled, though.

"Hey," one of them shouted, obviously thrilled, "this is like out of some movie." Right.

"Okay," I sort of muttered to myself, and I headed upstairs to the bathroom directly above in the history wing.

This time there were no greasers throttling any freshmen, and even if there had been they probably just would have bummed a few cigarettes off me and invited me to get high with them under the school. I scrubbed my hands for a few minutes with that powdered sort of soap they have in school bathrooms. It did a pretty good job.

The mirror over the sink was graffitied with black Sharpie: initials, Gilliard slurs, shit like that. Gilliard has an ass shaped like a UPS truck; it's kind of the fodder for a lot of graffiti.

I stared through all the ink and dried phlegm at my eyes' reflection. They were practically closed, and dark bags—almost purple—hung below them. If I didn't know better, I'd believe I'd been in a minor brawl. The flickering whiter-than-white lights cast shadows of my brow and nose down my face, and my pale skin looked paler than normal. My freckles still had summer depth, and a few near my upper lip were especially dark and sort of odd. They gave me a little snarl, or, if I squinted or stared long enough, they were crusty spots of blood where my lip had been split by the same hard-asses who blacked my eyes.

And my eyes. They looked heavy and deep, and dark in the middle. And just outside the black center they were red. And beyond that brown and green. And as I stared the black center grew. It threatened to engulf the other colors completely, so I leaned in toward the mirror, farther and farther, until my nose touched the dirty glass.

"Dude, what the hell are you doing?"

Fucking hell. I could see just enough of the room—in the mirror I was practically making out with—to spot Danny Goodman taking a piss behind me.

"Fuck off, Goody."

"You're insane. You know that, right, Fisher?"

Maybe I am, prick. I thought it to myself, and then I said it out loud. "Maybe I am, prick." I turned on the cold tap and splashed my face—haphazardly, so it went all over my shirt and the floor.

"Idiot," mumbled Goody as he left the bathroom.

"Dude, wash your hands!" I called after him, with my best Goodman hippie-fuck accent. To hear him and his idiot friends you'd think they just parked the fucking Woody outside after a day surfing off Venice Beach or someplace like that. Probably never left Long Island, really.

I dried off and gave myself a smirk in the mirror before heading back to Rohan's class. He was talking about "Hands."

"Welcome back, Simon." I'd been gone a while. I wondered for a minute how long I'd stood there staring at myself.

"Sorry. I scrubbed and scrubbed."

A whisper from my left: "'Out, damn spot,' eh, Simon?" What's this? Shakespeare-rooted wit from a fellow student? And a female one at that?

I gave a polite chuckle in reply, something I'm fairly sure I'd never done before that moment. Weird thing is,

I'm usually a closet-fan of horrible lit jokes. The chuckle could have been genuine if I hadn't stalled thinking about it—thinking, *Why the hell is Melanie Siegel talking to me? Is this some cruel junior-high-style mock job?*

It's not like I'd never spoken to Melanie before or anything, just to be clear. I was even on the track team with her in junior high, and for the fifteen seconds I was on the team freshman year, too; I had admired her not insignificant hotness. I don't think she could have been all that fond of me, though, once Lily and I started ditching practice runs to go smoke cigarettes together, though.

Melanie didn't say another word to me during class. She just sat there taking notes and hanging on Rohan's every word, looking sort of stuckup and oddly desirable in the process. I spent the next thirty minutes sneaking glances out of the corner of my eye and dwelling on her joke, and what it might have meant, if anything, which it probably didn't. I didn't hear a word of Rohan's hyper lecture on *Winesburg, Ohio*, which was fine, since the book's about as subtle as a mallet to the skull and doesn't really require in-depth analysis and open discussion. I was considering raising my hand and saying so when the buzzer rang.

Everyone shuffled out the door and into the crowded hallway. I wanted to talk to Rohan so I stayed behind. "Are we meeting today?"

"Don't we always on Thursdays?" He didn't look up from his notes.

"Right. Yeah." I picked at the ink stain on my right palm. "I wrote a lot."

He kept looking at his notes.

"I don't think you're going to like it."

"Why's that, Simon?" Very uninterested. Shit, what the hell crawled up your butt this morning?

"It's pretty weird stuff."

"Well, try writing sober some time."

I couldn't believe he actually said that.

"I was sober," I said after a few minutes. "And fuck you." Then I dropped *Winesburg, Ohio* on his desk and left the room. Maybe he finally looked up from his attendance book, but I wouldn't count on it.

"Feeling any better?"

Some greeting. Rohan was sitting at our regular table in the English study lounge when I got there after ninth period. I sat down across from him and pulled out my notebook and about thirty pages of nonsense. I slid the packet across the table to him.

He glanced at the first page, maybe skimmed the first few run-on sentences, then looked up at me. "What's on your mind, Simon?"

"Nothing."

"I believe it." Ha, ha. He kept reading the first page, flipped to the second, mumbled an occasional "hm," and went on to the third page. He was reading it only slightly faster than I'd written it. "What I can make out here is pretty heavy stuff. I don't know if you realize it, but you're going much deeper." Well, bully for me.

"It's not a story at all," I said, wanting to say something more. "It's just what I was thinking."

"I see that," he cracked, and he flipped through the remaining pages quickly. "You know I hate this stuff, but you do seem to be getting better at it." Love those backhanded compliments. "'Dark, dark eyes and sugary lips, spotted and curled. Twisting through words, and sounds come out—they strike me like air. Not a hint among them, when so much is happening, and I can just sit in my mud and splash my tantrum and think of her.' That's very poetic—sexual."

"Sexual?" I dropped my eyebrows and shot him an *are you sure?* glare.

"'Sugary lips'—hard to get less subtle than that, Simon." He started flipping through the pages, I guess looking for some other naughty parts.

"It's not about sex." I spoke pretty quietly. I felt like I'd said something horrible. My stomach jumped and fell. For some reason my temples started to ache, and I realized I was clenching my jaw. Shit, not now.

Rohan put down the packet of ramblings and looked at me. He pulled off his glasses as though he couldn't see me well enough. "What's it about to you?" Like it's open for debate.

"It's about my dad." Tighter. "That part you read is about my sister, and missing her. It's not sexual."

"The mud tantrum . . . that's about your sister, too?"

Jesus, I didn't come here for this. "No, it's about me being frustrated and pissed."

"About your sister?"

"No." I finally looked in his eyes, really stared him down, grit my teeth, and tried to fight it out with him, eye to eye, soul to soul, my burgeoning strength to his sickening analytical curiosity. And he looked away. It wasn't how I wanted to win this, I knew—like it was some juvenile staring contest—so I grabbed his pen and the packet of paper and scribbled in big red letters what I couldn't say out loud. I slid the packet back to him. That's how I wanted to win—with him feeling shittier than I did. So I grabbed my bag and watched a big tear as it dropped and stained the military green fabric a dark olive, and I walked out of the lounge. I'm a cruel fucking bastard.

| chapter 9 |

Noah and Lily were camped out in their usual spot out front. I saw them through the big windows as I huffed along the main hall—Lily with her butt parked on the yellow curb and Noah leaning on the brick pillar beside her. And they weren't alone, which isn't as uncommon as it sounds. Goody was there too, I guess buying some weed from Noah, or anyway setting up a buy for later on. It occurred to me that Noah was probably inviting him over to his palatial estate, maybe even planning a full-on party with his parents out of town. Moron. That's a guaranteed whooping from dear old Dad.

I almost wanted to say hi to Lily, but I detoured anyway, back around the main hall, past the cafeteria, and out the rarely-used auditorium exit. Mr. Freeman was blocking the door.

"Hi, Simon." Mr. Freeman was sort of overweight, at least for what you'd expect of a track coach. He wasn't much taller than me, and his hair was still brown, or what was left of it was. He had a whistle around his neck and a clipboard under his arm—incredibly typical. He loved that. I think the second last period ended, he'd slip on the Bulldog sweats, throw the whistle over his head, and grab the clipboard. It sure seemed like his next move most days would be looking for me. I pulled my Yankee cap out of my back pocket and slapped it onto my head.

"Hi, Mr. Freeman." I tugged at the brim of my hat, tightening the curve and blocking my eyes, which must have been pretty red and swollen. He just would have thought I was high or something.

"I've still got a place for you on the team, you know." I nodded wildly, hoping to end the conversation by showing what a rush I was in. "We're starting spring team practices today."

"I don't know, Mr. Freeman. I've been pretty busy. I'm probably pretty out of shape, too."

He looked at me like I'd died—he felt so sorry for me.

"All right, Simon. Think about it anyway, okay?" He glanced at his watch and walked toward the back of the school, toward the track. I imagined all the runners lined up along the fence by the infield, in their sweats, leaning and stretching—not a smile among them, like it was very urgent stuff, stretching. Pulling off my hat, I turned to leave, finally.

I swung the big black exit door violently open, hoping to bask in the drama of afternoon sunlight blinding me as I stepped outside. Instead I was met with a "What the fuck?" and a glare.

"Oh, shit. Sorry." It was Melanie. She'd been squatting against the wall right beside the door and it must have banged her knee when I swung it open.

"Well, be a little careful, all right, Simon?" She'd gotten to her feet and was rubbing her knee. It would bruise. Black and blue and purple. Maybe brown and green after a couple of days. As she bent slightly to reach her knee, her jaw-length light-brown hair fell lightly over her face. Made her look sort of pissed—but beautiful. She stood up straight and ran her hand through her hair, pushing it back and away from her eyes. She was dressed head to toe in navy and white oversized school-issued sweats, the number 52 on her thigh and the word "Bulldogs" across her sweatshirt-muted chest. Seriously, one thing I know about the world: there are tits *everywhere.*

"I'm sorry. Really. I was angry, and I . . ." I realized I'd only stopped crying a few minutes before. My eyes were red and dark. Hers suddenly went soft and light. They looked moist, but not sad. She knew I'd been crying.

"It's okay. It didn't really hurt that much—you just sort of scared me a little." And she put her hand on my shoulder. Made me feel about a foot tall.

"Sorry." I dropped my stare to the pavement. "Look, I have to go. My sister's leaving for school soon, and I want to see her before she leaves."

"Okay. I have to get to practice anyway," she said, forcing a little smile. "I'll see you in English tomorrow."

I nodded and walked off. God, was it good to get away from her. I couldn't handle that pity. I really wanted to take it all, absorb it into my skin, bask in it, huddle up against it and sleep, but it seemed too hard.

Noah and Lily were still hanging around out front. They didn't notice me walking down on the other side of the maintenance building or walking across 25A. I didn't pause at the Gap, and I didn't sit on the path across the parking lot to smoke. I went straight home. Suzanne was already packed; her bags sat by the front door where we normally put our shoes.

"Simon?" she called from upstairs. "Is that you?"

"Yeah."

She stuck her head out from the top of the stairs. "How was school?"

"Oh, wonderful."

"I bet."

"Aren't Mom and Dad home yet?" I strolled into the kitchen to look for signs of motherhood.

"No, Dad's got the long chemo today." They'd worked out this schedule so that every other session was like a full-time job. They'd have all been full-time, but I guess a patient can't handle that kind of assault.

I opened the fridge and pulled out the OJ just as Suzanne came up behind me and threw her arms around me in a bear hug. "I gotta go, Simon." She gave me a peck on the cheek and released me.

"Already?" She'd left the kitchen. I heard her opening the storm door and dragging a bag across the threshold, so I went to the door holding my juice to watch her toss the bag into the trunk of her friend's car. "Aren't you going to wait for Mom and Dad to get back?"

"I can't," she said as she snuck past me and grabbed her other bag. "They won't be back before eight or nine tonight, and we'd like to be up in Boston before that."

I muttered my comprehension through the upturned and emptied glass covering my mouth. She tossed the second bag in with the first, closed the trunk, and ran back to the door.

"I'll talk to you soon." I realized she didn't lean over to say it. I was taller than her. "You're okay?"

"Yeah, I'm fine," I said, a little "obviously" in my tone.

"Okay," with another peck on the cheek. "Miss you."

"Bye," I called coolly. Suzanne hopped across the lawn and into the passenger seat. She waved as the car drove off and around the curve toward the entrance to our expressway.

After quickly scribbling a note to my parents, I went out the back way and hopped the fence. The grassy slope isn't as green as I'd like it to be. It's been trod for years, by kids like me—half-sliding, half-walking—to reach the expressway, a good shortcut if you know how to use it. I guess most kids only walked a little ways down, to the first overpass. There were always plenty of beer cans and liquor bottles and cigarette butts. I stopped there that afternoon and leaned on the wall, right against some dipshit's tag. I used to sit there quite a bit, sometimes to write, sometimes to smoke, and sometimes just to enjoy the company speeding by—cars and trucks driven by faceless people. They'd zoom by, not even noticing I was there. I guess they didn't notice much of anything, like the dirty pigeons nesting and crapping, the slimy green growth over our heads, or the gray-green water that would drip and leave tiny stalactites above. It must have taken forever for those to form. Those icicles of suburban waste had seen so many kids like me sitting here.

So I sat there, enjoying a few cigarettes and almost wishing I had some weed, until the sun had set completely. The traffic thinned meanwhile, and I knew my parents had already come home to an empty house and a curt note on the fridge. I dropped my last butt and climbed to my feet. For a moment I considered just heading home, but a little restlessness got the better of me.

Instead of going back up through my backyard and to Noah's house, I walked on the shoulder of the expressway. If you go that way, you can get from my house to Noah's side of the Heights in about five minutes. That night it took me one cigarette to get halfway, and then I just sang to myself to pass the rest of the time. While I walked, as I sang and hummed "He Feels Bad," I remembered one Thursday night Suzanne came home after curfew. It was about one. She'd gone into New York to see Helmet and came in sort of rowdy I guess. She woke me up when she knocked something over downstairs, and then I heard Dad reading her the riot act. I think she was drunk. I lay there in the dark listening for a while; Dad's booming voice made me shake every time it was his turn to scream. I couldn't hear Suzanne or my mom at all.

After a while, I guess after everyone had screamed the fear out of themselves, I heard my mom come back upstairs, then my dad, and then Suzanne tapped on my door. She pushed it opened and closed it quietly behind her. "Simon?" she whispered. "Are you awake?"

I lifted my head a little, pulled it out from under the blanket, and mumbled.

"Good." She sat down near my feet and put her hand on my ankle. "Sorry I made so much noise."

"'Sokay," I peeped, and lowered my head. "Are you drunk?"

"A little bit." She rubbed my foot. The moonlight through my window caught her eyes and they shone for a moment until she leaned toward me and forced a little smile. "But don't worry. It's not going to be a major deal, okay? Dad's all right."

"Okay."

"Will you give me a hug?" She slid along the side of the bed and opened her arms to me. I felt her breath on my face. It was warm and smelled of beer. "I feel bad."

"Okay," I said, and she leaned over, picked up my shoulders in her arms, and squeezed.

"I love you." A peck on the cheek.

"I know."

"Go to sleep now."

"I will."

"Good night, Simon." Another kiss on the cheek.

"G'night."

"Hey, Simon!" Noah was a mile high when I got to his house. It wasn't a full-on party—just Noah and Lily and Goody and a few other serious smokers.

"Hey." That restlessness I'd felt faded pretty quickly as I stepped past Noah. I moseyed down to the basement living room where the little crew was congregated, zombie-ing the TV and otherwise doing very little. Everyone turned around slowly and hey'ed me. I returned the favor and went to sit with Lily on the floor.

"Hi, Simon." She looked pretty down.

"You're high as shit, huh?" Her eyes were nearly closed.

"Yeah, I'm pretty wasted, Simon." She was drunk, too. Looked a bit green. She dropped her head into my lap and groaned. "Did your sister leave?"

"A few hours ago." I kept my eyes on the TV.

"Do you miss her?"

"No. She just left."

Noah threw himself into the couch nearest my head and leaned a bong into my face. "It's amazing shit, man."

I tried to give him a sort of cold look. "Do you have any beer?"

"Oh, man, you gotta take a hit first."

"Later. I just want a beer right now." I looked back at the TV. Lily was looking up at me like a wounded puppy and Noah was staring at me like an open-mouthed bass.

Goody decided to chime in. "Dude, Fisher, just take a hit. You could use it." I was shocked to discover he was with it enough to comment. His buddies chuckled a little, which I guess egged him on.

"Yo, do you guys know what this freak was doing today?" He came completely back to earth just then and leaned forward into hilarious-story pose. "Seriously, I went into the boys' room during first period today, and this guy's kissing the mirror over the sink." While he talked he mimed a make-out scene with the air, apparently hamming up my performance from the bathroom. "Looked like a total freak."

He looked at me. "What the hell were you on this morning, Fisher?"

"Fuck you, Goody."

He chuckled and leaned back. "Say that to me again, Fisher. Go ahead." He smiled this thin, stoned smirk and closed his eyes.

People who are that high shouldn't threaten people who are sober and pissed. "All right." I didn't say it angry or intensely at all. I just said it: "Fuck you, Goody."

He tried to stand, real intimidating, but leaned too far and tripped on a Nintendo cord and fell right over the coffee table. Lily jumped to her feet and tripped a little. She landed next to Noah on the couch. Meanwhile Goody was struggling to his feet, and I got up. He leaped at me and pushed me into the kitchen, both of us stumbling. I threw a few punches but could only really reach his shoulders and back; I doubt I hurt him much. We hit the ground hard and my head hit the tiled floor. Within seconds, Noah had pulled Goody off of me, and Lily was kneeling beside me. I don't know how any of these guys cleared their heads enough to stop us so quickly.

Danny Goodman had been giving me pretty frequent shit since the seventh grade. I was shy and pretty puny, and he was already getting high back then and thought he was majorly hot shit. I hated him; everyone knew it. Lily was especially aware, I guess. You could tell because she'd get a little funny when Noah had Goody over. Noah probably hated Goody too, but he always tried to impress him and get him over to the house to hang out. Pretty pathetic.

I sat there on the kitchen floor while Goody got to his feet and staggered into the living room.

"Fuck you, Goody," I called after him, sort of laughing. Lily put a cold beer on my head. It wasn't all that bad, though, so I just took the beer from her and opened it.

"Simon, you're going to get a bump." Her voice was an octave higher than normal.

"I'm fine." I looked up at her face, and tears were streaming down her cheeks. She was pale and tired-looking—looked like absolute shit. "Do you wanna go throw up or something?"

I took a pretty long swig from the beer as she glared at me and got up. Sure enough, she headed to the bathroom and probably retched her brains out. I finished my beer and Noah gave me another one.

"What the fuck is wrong with you, Simon?" I'd embarrassed him in front of Goody, his platonic little crush.

By the time I collected myself and took a seat on the couch, Goody and his stupid friends had left, and Lily was sitting on the floor in front of the TV again and hugging her knees. She looked remotely cute.

"You feeling better?" I asked.

Lily looked up at me without moving—just lifted her eyes, brown. She didn't reply.

"You look better," I added.

She lowered her eyes again, then closed them. I glanced at the doorway to the kitchen. Noah was still cleaning up a little of the mess Goody and I had left in there. I moved off the couch and down on the floor with Lily.

"Seriously, Lil. You okay?"

She nodded. I put an arm around her shoulder and she leaned into me a little.

"Your nose is bleeding." I didn't remember getting hit in the nose at all, but she was right. It wasn't a gusher or anything, but there was blood on my fingers after I checked above my lips.

"Don't feel a thing."

"Tell me about it." She turned her eyes up to me and gave me a puppy-dog pout, so I kissed her. As she put her hand on my neck, then behind my head, I tasted my blood on her lips mingling with her makeup. She was right, though; I didn't feel much of anything.

"Holy shit." Noah had obviously finished cleaning up in the kitchen, and he came into the living room laughing and exclaiming. "I knew this would happen someday!"

Lily immediately pulled away from my face and blushed. She was smiling though as she took her hands off me and tucked her dark hair behind her ears.

"Well, shit, don't let me interrupt!" He left the room laughing and whooping, and a few minutes later I smelled burning weed coming from one of the other TV rooms. Noah's house has about seventeen TV rooms.

Lily and I sat on the floor, awkwardly, for a few minutes. She petted the short fuzzy hair on the back of my head as she leaned on my arm, and I moved my hand between her hip and waist, thinking about the curve. There wasn't much of one there, actually.

"You all right?" she asked, out of the blue.

"What do you mean? Sure. I'm fine."

"Noah's not gonna come back up, you know." She moved her hand to my neck and then around to the side of my face. I shrugged and sniffled. I do that sometimes, I guess, to cut the silence.

Lily shifted and got to her knees to face me, then moved in real close and started kissing me again. I kissed her back, and she took my hand and put it on her back, then leaned forward. She was on top of me and kissing me, and all I kept trying to do was keep up with the pace of her mouth. I was so tired and I wasn't really interested, so I just moved my hands on her back and the back of her head and tried to open and close my mouth at the right times. I wondered how long she'd want to do this.

She may have sensed that, because she gave one little sort of kiss and rolled off me. I have to admit she looked very cute—it's not like I'd never noticed before or anything. I mean, she's not gorgeous at all, but her mouth sometimes looks very cute. I got up on my side and moved her hair away from her face.

"Are you all right, Simon?"

"Why do you keep asking me that? I'm fine." I kept playing with her hair, so I wouldn't sound too jerky.

"Do you want me to leave?" She looked up at me and twisted her mouth, in that way that makes her pretty cute. I didn't know what to say—started feeling guilty about being in a bad mood. So I just leaned over her and kissed her again, mainly to make her stop asking me these questions. It seemed to do the trick; she threw her arms around my neck and kissed me all over my face. Her tears and makeup, and my blood, stained her face and mouth. It made her look beautiful. I never told her so.

"I'm really tired, Lil."

"Do you want to go home?" She said it like it would have meant the end of the world or something.

"No, I left my folks a note saying I'd be staying here tonight."

"On a Thursday night?" The deep sadness immediately vanished from her voice, replaced by the typical Lily bewilderment. "Won't they be annoyed?"

"Nah." Actually, though, I hadn't even thought about what day it was. For a minute I wondered if my inadvertent attempt to break new ground by staying at Noah's on a school night would be successful, but quickly realized I didn't care much. "I'm going to sleep."

"Okay."

"In the guest room." I stood up, wondering if she'd try to join me. She sat up, but stayed on the rug. "Good night."

Noah's house has only one guest room. It's on the other side of the kitchen and is probably really the maid's quarters, but his family doesn't have a maid. I walked slowly down the hall as I called good night to Noah. He called back through a thin, nasty cough. I kicked off my sneakers, pulled off my jeans, and took off my sweater, before climbing into bed in my boxers and System of a Down T. I don't know what made me do it, but I also made sure the door was opened a crack.

| chapter 10 |

I woke up to a few solid bangs on the guest room door. Lily was sleeping next to me, with her arm over my chest and her face pointed away from me—looked very uncomfortable. The blankets were pushed down to my hips. I honestly didn't remember her getting into bed at all. Her jeans were off, though, and I looked down at her underwear. There were little monkeys on it.

"Wake, up, guys. First period in thirty. We got time for a quick wake and bake!"

Lily stirred and faced me. She still had smeared makeup on her face, and her hair was knotted and greasy. I pushed it away from her eyes and behind her ears.

She smiled huge and kissed me gently on the lips before stretching and sitting up. "Simon, I am so dead." She was still smiling though.

"Dead?"

"My parents have no idea where I am," she said, picking up her jeans off the floor. All her jeans are like the girl versions of the sort I buy. They're baggy and all that, but they also have like a stripe up the legs or some glittery shit on the ass pockets or something. Cute-core, I guess. "They probably called the police already."

Lily's parents got divorced right before I met her, just before junior high. That's how I met her: The elementary schools from the Heights and the Hills combined into the bigger junior high, and Lily was in my homeroom and my history class. She was probably sitting right behind me when I left the room the day my grandpa died. Anyway, even though her parents had been divorced for like four years, she still talked like they lived together, even though she only saw her dad a few times a month on the weekends.

I watched her as she sat at the foot of the bed and pulled on her jeans and her T-shirt. I couldn't keep my eyes off her bra-strap; it looked so ridiculous to me, like a little girl playing dress-up. I also caught the profile of her tits; they made her look uncomfortable, like a little boy forced to wear a suit and tie to his distant uncle's funeral.

"You guys want any of this or what?" Noah was getting impatient, so I put on my jeans and walked into the kitchen.

"Hey."

"Hey, Simon!" He came at me for a high five, like I was the returning conqueror or something. What a jerk. "You want some of this?" He stuck a glass bowl in my face.

"No, how about some juice?"

"Oh man, Simon, what the fuck?" He was actually getting pissed at me for not smoking with him in so long. Ridiculous. Lily came into the kitchen, pulling on her sweater, just in time.

"Morning," she chirped. Man, did she look happy. She went to the fridge and helped herself to some juice, then gave me her glass to finish. It was very cute. I guess we became an instant couple.

Noah turned his back on both of us and lowered his head. "Lily, you could take a shower if you want," he said in his coolest voice, and he left the room.

"What's wrong with him?" Lily came up behind me and wrapped her arms around my neck. I closed my eyes and basked in it for a second. I mean, it totally reminded me of my big sister, which was pretty weird I guess.

"I won't get high with him anymore."

"Why not?" She kissed my ear.

"Don't want to."

I felt her shrug. "Okay." She released her hug and started out of the kitchen. "I'm gonna take a hit and a shower," she said over her shoulder. I watched her butt as she left the kitchen, and a few minutes later I heard the vague sounds of water moving through the pipes.

Noah was sulking in front of some morning show when I sat next to him on the couch. Some ridiculously hot blond chick was explaining how to deal with relatives over the upcoming holidays. Noah was telling her to fuck off. Someone needs to talk to that guy.

DECEMBER 15

Her back to me,
Arched and weighed down.
Dark hair in a band,
Leaving her shoulders bare.
She shivered.

I would have reached for her,
Touched her shoulders, her back.
But my hands are cold.

| chapter 11 |

I never thought much would change with Lily being my girlfriend. I mean, she and Noah were the only people I hung out with much anyway, so now I'd be kissing her and fondling her and she'd be kissing me and fondling me. Not much of a difference, really. Even Noah didn't seem to care much anymore after that first morning. Actually, he wasn't around as much after that. He spent most of his high-time with Goody and those jerks. I still walked to school with him, but I think he felt pretty awkward about it most of the time, which I thought was hilarious—like there was some horrible past between us. Ooh, I don't get high anymore. Definitely feel rejected, Noah, you dipshit.

By New Year's Eve, everything was starting to look pretty good. There's this thing called a "T-count." I'm not sure what the "T" stands for, but I hope it's not "tumor," because that would be way too blunt. Anyway, the point is my dad's T-count had started dropping a lot, from like a thousand to seventy or something outrageous like that. His doctor he was seeing, the genius my uncle Abe came up with, thought that was great, and my parents had meetings with him or his assistant in Manhattan constantly. It wouldn't be too much longer before they could do some surgery and get rid of the remaining cancer.

My two favorite faculty members had been pretty bearable too. Rohan had said he was sorry about my dad after my miniature tantrum, so our meetings were much easier, if a bit awkward, and I'd agreed to meet with Freeman about the spring team right after break. That meant I'd miss the first two weeks of practice, but he didn't seem to mind much when I explained my situation. He put his head back a little and looked down at me, then put his hand on my shoulder, like he was a rabbi or something. "Take as long as you need, Simon. Practices can go on without the Flying Fisher for a little while, eh?"

I don't know what changed my mind about the track team. The simple answer is Melanie, looking unbearably cute in her track sweats. Of course, I was with Lily, so it's not like I was really interested or anything. I think it was more for my dad, actually. I knew he'd be psyched to see me running again, and if I quit smoking because of it he'd be ecstatic.

Suzanne was back home for a few weeks too. Mom and Dad were eternally beaming, it seemed, with both of us around the house. And since the chemo was going so well and Dad was getting a little stronger, there hadn't been another death-talk since I'd walked out on the first one. Lily and I were getting pretty comfortable, too. I mean, it was sort of one-sided, I guess. Like, she would always grab on me in the halls at school, and she would call me every night and all that, but really that's always how we'd been, Lily and me. She was always way more into it overall.

Lily's mom left her alone on New Year's Eve; she was on some cruise that left from Miami that day. My folks went to this party their friends were throwing; normally my folks threw it, but since Dad was feeling pretty unwell still, some other couple volunteered to host. I was sure my folks wouldn't stay long, and Suzanne went into Manhattan to see some friends from Boston, so I had her drop me off at Lily's.

"So," she snickered as we pulled up to Lily's house. "This *is* your girlfriend's house?" I remembered that Suzanne had asked about Lily before, and I blushed a little.

Suzanne reached into the back seat and grabbed a brown bag. She handed it to me. "Here. Happy New Year."

I peeked into the bag. Champagne. "Thanks."

"No sweat, Simon," she said with a wink. "Be careful when you throw out that bag, though. There's something else at the bottom."

"What?"

She just smiled at me and gave me a kiss on the cheek. "Have fun. I'll see you, um, eventually."

"Thanks. You too." The paper bag was wet and cold, and as I walked up the lawn and dropped the knocker, I realized I was nervous. I hadn't been nervous even once around Lily. And that just made me more nervous.

Lily opened the door. I nearly dropped the bag at her feet as she grabbed my wrist and pulled me inside. She'd done up the living room with candles and shit, and there was this glorious looking dinner set up on the coffee table. She stood beside it and beamed. "It's all Zen Palate, Simon." That's my favorite vegetarian place.

"It looks great," I managed to stutter. She smiled and bit her lower lip. I remembered the brown paper bag I was sweating all over. "Oh, um, Suzanne got this for us." I pulled out the bottle. It was wet with condensation. I held it out to Lily. Something was clinging to the bottom of the bottle. It fell, and Lily bent to pick it up just as I saw what it was.

"Whoa." That was the best I could do in that situation: "whoa."

Lily sort of quivered as she stared at the vacuum-sealed disc in her palm. In my defense, the only thing she could come up with to say was "um."

We hadn't had sex yet. Honestly I hadn't had sex yet with anyone. I don't know why Suzanne decided to slip a goddamn rubber in the bag with the champagne. I assume she wasn't being cruel, since she never is, but I still thought it was weird. "I swear to God, Lil, Suzanne put that in there."

She nodded. "Okay." She got up off the couch and finally stopped staring at the thing. "I'm gonna put it away, I guess."

I decided I'd better have the champagne opened by the time she got back. Pretty tricky business, opening champagne. I got a little on my shirt and nearly caused a fire knocking over one of her candles. While trying to decide if the cups on the table were good enough for champagne, I realized this was not how I'd pictured New Year's Eve with Lily. I wanted to sit with her in front of the TV, eat some Taco Bell, make out a little, and stay up late. I wanted to kiss her at midnight, maybe do a little more than that, and then sleep in her bed with her head on my chest. I didn't want any sort of romantic dinner, any candles, any high stakes. I poured the champagne and drank a glass, then refilled it and sat on the couch, waiting for Lily to come back.

"Are you hungry?" She showed up without a smile.

"Sure. It smells awesome."

She took a seat on the floor beside the coffee table, so I sat down next to her. We ate without saying much, and we finished the champagne by the time most of the food was gone. I couldn't keep my eyes off her, though. She looked really scared, like her plans to have this grown-up New Year's Eve had sort of gotten away from her and she didn't like where things were headed. I took her hand and she looked up at me.

"Are you okay?" I asked, making it pretty clear that for once I was asking her, instead of the other way around. She loved asking me if I was okay.

She nodded. I kissed her once, then again.

She lowered her eyes and said, "I threw it out."

"What?"

"I threw out the condom."

"Good."

She smiled at me, finally, and squeezed my hand. "I rented a few movies," she said, real quiet. I tried to remember if Lily had always looked on the verge of tears, and decided she had. Probably her melodramatic streak.

As we sat down in front of the TV and Lily leaned on my arm, I felt all that anxiousness slip away. We watched three horrible horror movies and laughed a lot, and we didn't even notice when midnight came and went. At around two in the morning, Lily started dozing off. I snuck out from under her and turned off the TV. She woke up long enough for us to make it upstairs to her room.

Lily let herself fall backwards onto her bed and curled up with her knees against her chest. I curled up behind her and pet her hair until she fell asleep. I fell asleep pretty quickly after her.

It's not a great position to fall asleep, though. I woke up just an hour or so later, I think, and my arm was totally numb. I didn't have much experience with spooning, so maybe I was doing it wrong, but it was really uncomfortable. I slowly and quietly sat up and started pulling off my sneakers. Lily shifted behind me and then rolled over onto her stomach.

As I was unbuttoning my jeans, I glanced at the trash can next to Lily's desk. The condom was sitting right on top, and I thought of Suzanne, and the only experience I actually have with spooning. Sometimes, when I was much younger, after my dad had lost his temper in a big way, and I'd been crying, Suzanne would come into my room. I'd have the lights off and the blankets up over my head, curled up in my bed. Suzanne would whisper my name and feel her way over to the bed. She'd lie down next to me and curl up too, then she'd put one arm over me and squeeze me tight while kissing me gently on the back of my neck. I'd feel so much better. Sometimes she'd stay there all night, and I'd sleep with my head on her shoulder, or sometimes she'd try to make me laugh, and would tickle me until I couldn't be sad anymore if I wanted to. My mom used to think I did want to, actually. Be sad, I mean. I still don't know what she meant by that.

I turned around and lightly tapped Lily on the shoulder. She rolled over.

"Do you want to sleep in your clothes, Lil?" I whispered. I felt like Suzanne, trying to take care of her or something. Lily shook her head a little.

"Okay, I'm going to take off your shoes and your jeans, all right?" She nodded and smiled, her eyes still closed.

I slipped off her sneakers and pulled off her socks. She hummed while I did, and lifted her arms over her head, making her T-shirt go up and expose her stomach and the top of her jeans. I unbuttoned them, and pulled down the zipper, then stood up and pulled them off by the ankles. I have to admit, she looked pretty good lying there, so I'm glad she never opened her eyes; I was probably sporting some major wood. Anyway, she shook, so I lay down next to her, pulled her on top of me, and then pulled the blanket over both of us. She kissed my cheek.

"I love you, Simon." I barely heard it, she said it so softly, as though she thought she'd said it in her dream, and then she fell asleep. I felt every slow, warm breath on my neck, trying to decide if I felt the same way and doubting it. We woke late on the first of year, and, before Lily showered, I kissed her good morning and good-bye. Her lips were always much softer in the morning, right after she woke up.

| chapter 12 |

The first day of school came too quickly. I'd been trying not to smoke too much, mainly because I didn't want to look like a hack at my first track practice. I met with Freeman after school the first day back.

"Thanks for coming down, Simon." He looked absolutely thrilled to see me.

"Sure." I sat across from him, the coaches' desk between us, in the equipment room. Every coach used the same desk, so there was really nothing on it. "Just so you know, I'll have to be late to practice twice a week, on account of my meetings with Mr. Rohan, you know, for my independent study project."

He twisted up his face and leaned forward a little. "What sort of project? I didn't know you were involved in anything like that."

"Oh, it's not a very big deal. Just some writing I've been doing."

He leaned back again, considering the situation. "Well," he said after a minute, "if it can't be helped, it can't be helped. You need to consider that high school transcript, I suppose. Those extracurricular activities are very impressive." Oh, right. That's just what I was thinking.

"So," he announced, getting back to the point, "we won't go through the whole tryouts process, obviously, since I know what you're capable of and the season starts in less than two weeks." He picked up a brown paper package, like something out of a butcher shop, from the floor beside him and placed it on the desk in front of me. "There's your team sweats. You're number"—he flipped through the few papers on his clipboard—"thirty-three."

"Okay." I took the package off the desk and set it in my lap.

He continued looking through his papers for a few minutes, then looked up at me. "Well, go ahead and get changed. Practice starts in twenty minutes. You can get stretching up by the track. Everyone else is probably already up there."

"Right." I went to my locker and sat in front of it on the old wooden bench, the paper package in my lap, for several minutes. Back in junior high, Lily was on track with me for two years. She quit before I did, but wasn't missed all that much. Actually, she hardly ever competed at meets. That's when I really got to know her, though.

During the long runs on seventh-grade spring track, Lily and I would sneak off to the back of the school and hang out on the swing set by the connected day-care center.

Back then, Lily wasn't into any good music at all. I don't even remember what crap she was listening to, but I would ramble on about bands I thought she should listen to, and within a few days she'd always know the album backwards and forwards. I'd say things like, "You oughtta check out Kittie. I bet you'd like them a lot. They recorded their first CD when they were like fifteen or something," and she'd just sit there swinging slowly and grinning at me. I don't think she was all that cute back then, but she was a breeze to hang out with.

Eventually, I tore open the paper and pulled out my sweats. The team shorts and tank top were in there too. I hated that uniform. It always smelled like the Salvation Army racks, and there are no guys who could look hetero wearing it. I tossed it into my locker, along with my jeans and hooded sweatshirt, and just put the sweats on over my regular T-shirt and boxers. You could get away with that until the weather started to warm up. After that, you had to wear the proper uniform every practice.

Sure enough, by the time I got up to the track, about twenty-five kids were stretching and doing quick sprints and shit. A few kids who I knew from the junior high team watched me as I walked up, obviously surprised to see me. The seniors, who had no idea who I was, I guess, glanced at me with annoyed faces. Melanie waved. I waved back and took a spot on the fence to stretch. Within a minute or so, Freeman was blowing his whistle. Everyone turned around and leaned on the fence, facing him.

"Okay, so, before our warm-up run, I think most of you know Simon Fisher." He motioned toward me with his clipboard. "He hasn't been with us for a couple of years or so, but let's all hope he hasn't lost his knack, okay?" I let myself smile sarcastically, and noticed Melanie smiling pretty sincerely out of the corner of my eye.

Freeman gave his whistle another blow. "Okay, one mile," he barked. "Slowly, Siegel!" A few people chuckled, and Melanie laughed and rolled her eyes. I assumed she was still our long distance rabbit—a short distance runner who tempts the other team's long-distancers to start too fast—as I took off down the long stretch of the track, in a lazy trot.

It turned out to be a very slow mile. I let myself finish toward the back, just ahead of a couple of freshmen. Melanie, of course, finished at the front, with Robin, miling star of the junior high team and consummate swirly victim. Even with my smoking, though, it wasn't much of a challenge to finish without being winded. I was starting to think this wouldn't be a problem at all when Freeman announced event split-offs.

"Two- and four-hundred-yarders, with Scott." Melanie, a freshman girl, and a tall senior headed off to the opposite long-stretch of the track. "That's you, Simon." Oh, right.

I hustled to catch up to the group. Melanie hung back for me.

"So, you're back on the team, eh, Simon?"

"I guess so." I watched the ground as we cut across the grass of the infield.

"It's a good thing. Our only 200-yarder is Rebecca since I decided to focus on the 400." She motioned to the freshman with her head and leaned toward my ear. "She's not very good," she whispered. I felt her breath on my ear and a chill ran up my spine. Very typical.

"What about this senior? That's Scott?" I didn't really care, actually. Just felt like I ought to say something.

"Yeah, he's the boys' captain. Runs the 400 with me."

We reached the opposite straightaway, and Melanie started doing some more stretching.

Scott seemed like a very well-adjusted, charming, handsome son of a bitch. My prick alarm was ringing four alarms.

"Simon Fisher, right?" Scott offered me his hand, and I shook it. God, seniors can be pompous.

"Yeah."

"Freeman tells me you're a 200 natural."

I shrugged.

"You warmed up?"

"Sure."

"All right then," he said, setting up a few sets of starting blocks.

"My start's probably a little rusty," I said, hoping he wasn't planning on throwing me right into it again. He was.

"I know. Let's give it one shot, though, okay?" He put his feet into a set of blocks and planted his hands in front of him.

"Against you?"

Melanie smiled, and the freshman girl set up on the third set of blocks.

"Sure," said Scott. "I've got to set a pace for you, you know?"

I shrugged again and awkwardly got myself into position on the inside blocks. The 200-yard run only takes one curve, so the blocks are staggered. I could see Scott and Rebecca in front of me. She had a very cute ass. Best thing about the track team, by the way.

Melanie stayed along the infield fence and raised her arm. God, it had been awhile since I felt like that: All this pressure builds up in your chest and your head lightens a little as you crouch there watching and waiting for the start, like someone had just challenged you to a fight. Finally, Melanie dropped her hand, and I kicked off the blocks.

Starting on the inside in the 200 is a major plus. As you push off, you see your opponents' starts, and they're rarely perfect. Scott's was good, probably as good as mine, but Rebecca's was tragic. She was practically standing straight up by the time she got moving. The other benefit is you've got all your opponents in front of you. You have to catch them, and that's all you can think of. In a race that short, that's a helpful way to think, since it's far too short to burn out.

By the time we came out of the curve and reached the hundred or so yards of straightaway, I'd passed Rebecca and was almost even with Scott. He obviously wasn't a 200-yard runner; he was keeping a 400-yard pace. I wondered if he'd kick at all, then showed him mine. I have a pretty good kick. The 200-yard kick is subtle, since it's such a short race. I caught him and even got a few paces past him by the time he really started chugging. He crossed first, but only by a leg. I think if he weren't so tall, I would've won.

They always tell you to keep moving after a race, so you don't tighten up, but I was a mess. My chest hurt—I could barely breathe. I didn't get it; I'd felt fine during the warm-up and the race, but I thought I was going to die as I leaned over with my hands on my knees, gasping for breath and wanting to puke. Melanie, who had jogged through the infield to meet us, started rubbing my back and offering me water. I shook my head and coughed a little.

"Walk a little, Simon."

I nodded and tried my best to pace around. Scott, meanwhile, the pompous idiot, was trying to shake my hand, like it was the goddamn Olympics or something. I nodded at him and gave him a very limp shake before collapsing onto the infield lawn.

Melanie sort of laughed at me. "Want a cigarette?" She was leaning on the infield fence, watching me die on the lawn.

Between gasps and coughs, I gave her a very sarcastic "ha, ha," and after a few minutes, she took my hand and I got to my feet. Very friendly girl.

Scott called over Mr. Freeman. He showed up tsk'ing how out of shape I was, but also obviously impressed I'd kept up with Scott.

"Mr. Freeman, did you recruit a smoker for my team?" I hate seniors. What an asshole.

"Apparently, yes, Scott." Freeman looked at me sideways. I suppose there's no way he would have known I was smoking now. "You're going to have to quit, Fisher." He wrote something in his notes. Reminded me of my dad's doctor. "If you don't, the only record you'll set this season is the shortest time between joining and being cut. Do I make myself clear?"

"Yes."

Melanie was still sort of laughing at me as the four of us—me, Melanie, Scott, and Rebecca—headed back to our starting blocks.

Practice didn't get much better after that. Every race I ran got worse and worse. Even Rebecca kept close at my heels by the end. By the time the warm-down came around, every breath burned. I walked down to the locker room feeling pretty much like shit. Melanie trotted up to my side.

"You're going to be a real pleasure to be around tomorrow, huh?" Man, could that girl smile. Made me twitch, in a good way.

"Maybe I'll sleep in," I said with a shrug, trying to copy her lighthearted sarcasm. It seemed to be her style. Of course, I didn't have any style, so I figured it would do.

"No, you won't," she said, changing her smile a bit and squinting like a sage. "Rohan will kill you, grasshopper. Besides, class is boring without you there to argue with him."

"I haven't done that in a long time," I said, defending myself, and my voice jumped an octave.

"I know. And it's been boring." She headed toward the girls' locker room. "I'll see you there!"

I smiled despite myself and waved as she jogged off. In the locker room, ignoring the other team members, I changed quickly and threw my sweats in my army bag to take home to wash. Lily was waiting for me when I walked outside. She offered me a cigarette.

"Where'd you get that?" I asked. Lily usually couldn't buy her own, since she was pretty small and had a very young face. "You didn't have to wait for me, you know."

"I know." She lowered her eyes a little, and we started walking toward 25A. "Noah got a pack for me today."

"What, you guys smoke up together or something?" I tried not to sound pissed about it, but I guess I was sort of.

Lily just shrugged, and I took the cigarette she was still offering. After one drag I thought I would puke so I dropped it.

"What's the matter with you?" she said, stopping.

I stopped a few feet passed her and turned to face her. "Nothing. I just didn't want it, that's all."

She squinted at me. Her eyes got a little wet. "I was watching you at practice today."

I looked at my feet. "Yeah?"

"Do you like that girl?"

"What girl?"

"Melanie Siegel." She said like she was spitting out a bad piece of chicken.

My heart jumped. "No."

"Really?" a tear slid down her cheek. Jesus, I nearly lost it myself.

"Really." I stood staring at her, my heart beating a mile a minute. She took a step toward me and I took her hand. She pulled her hand away and threw her arms around my waist. I hugged her back, and she squeezed me tight.

Her hair smelled like smoke. I tightened my hug and kissed her neck. She pulled away and smiled up at me. Her coat was open, and I could see her shirt with "Kittie" printed in those ornate gothic letters of theirs. I remembered the night she bought it. The three of us had gone into New York for the show, and Lily bought it the instant we entered the venue and wore it that night. Noah had told her to pull off the shirt she was wearing, smirking like he does whenever he makes comments about her tits, but she just put it on over her old shirt and gave him the finger.

"I got your shoulder all wet," she said. Tears were still on her cheeks.

"That's okay." And we walked on to the strip mall, holding hands, and split up there. Lily headed up to the Hills, while I went through the lot to the Heights. My mom greeted me at the door when I came in, and my dad called to me from the couch in the living room.

"Hey!" He was wearing jeans and his bathrobe. Of course, he hadn't been to work since the diagnosis. "How was practice?"

"Okay, I guess," I said, sitting next to him. He gave my knee a pat. "I did real well in the beginning, while I could still breathe."

My mom came and gave me kiss on the top of my head. "You smell like smoke," she said, in a sort of sing-song voice. Dad sighed.

"I only had like one drag, right after practice, and it was gross, so I put it out. I swear." Dad raised his eyebrows at me. "I swear. I hadn't had any today at all before that."

"Okay," he said, and my mom tsk'ed at me once before announcing dinner.

"Where's Suzanne?" I asked no one in particular.

"I think she's on the phone upstairs." He leaned closer to me, like a gossiping school girl. "With her boyfriend."

Suzanne walked into the living room a moment later. "What are you two talking about?" She smiled and plopped down on the couch next to me. Dad picked up the paper and cleared his throat.

"Oh, nothing, nothing," he said, and he winked at me.

Suzanne gave me a kiss on the cheek. "Hi, Simon."

"Hi." I sucked my teeth for a second. "So, you have a boyfriend?"

She opened her mouth, then curled it into a smile, before grabbing a pillow and tossing it at my dad. "No," she whined. "He's not my boyfriend." I thought of the condom she'd given me on New Year's Eve. It hadn't occurred to me before that it might have come from a box of them.

"I want to know when we get to meet this boy," my mom called from the kitchen. I helped my dad get up and the three of us went in for dinner. The newspapers had been given a new spot at the top of the basement steps, so Suzanne was across from me again.

"It's nothing serious," she continued as we ate. Mom had made pasta for me and chicken for everyone else. I'd decided not to eat meat anymore for a while. Lily's influence, I guess. Maybe guilt. "We've only hung out a few times."

"Well, you sure have been on the phone with him a lot since you got home," my mom said with a glance at me.

"What can I say," Suzanne quipped through a smile. "He can't get enough." She looked at me, and I smiled.

"I could understand that," said my mom, and she gave Suzanne a quick hug. I rolled my eyes and gave Suzanne a little kick under the table. She cocked her head at me, stuck out her tongue, and gave me the loser eyebrows. Finally.

"It's good to have you back, Suzie," I said, barely realizing I'd even opened my mouth.

She smiled at me for a second. "Wow. No one's called me that in years."

She was right, of course. She'd insisted, actually, on her thirteenth birthday. From that point on, after a short grace period, everyone called her Suzanne. For me, calling her Suzie meant a torturous tickle session, which occasionally wasn't so bad, really.

Mom and Dad beamed at both of us for an instant, until Suzanne, who has a gift for it, got us all laughing. "Well, that's it, Simon," she said with a straight face, off-handedly returning to her chicken. "You are getting majorly tickled tonight."

| chapter 13 |

After dinner, the four of us played a long two-on-two game of Trivial Pursuit, Suzanne and me versus Mom and Dad. We won by a mile, and then Mom announced she had to go upstairs to watch a movie on cable she'd been wanting to see. Dad said he'd rather chew aluminum foil than watch it, and he picked up the paper to work on the crossword puzzle. Suzanne and I sat together on the couch to watch some very brainless TV.

"So," she said during a commercial, patting my hand, "you never told me how your New Year's Eve went." She raised her eyebrows suggestively.

I shrugged and flipped through the five or six channels actually worth checking in on. "Fine." Of course, I knew what she was getting at, but I didn't much want to talk about it.

"Just fine?"

"Mm-hm."

"Nothing you want to tell me." I shook my head. "Nothing at all?"

I picked up a throw pillow from the couch and hugged it against my stomach. "Nothing happened, Suzanne. Or nothing like that, anyway."

"That's okay," she said after a moment, like I needed someone to tell me.

"I know it is." I stopped flipping around. "We just didn't want to."

"That's okay, too."

"I know it is."

She looked over at me and smiled weakly.

"What?" I said, looking back at the TV and starting to cycle through the channels again.

"Nothing." She kept staring at me. "You're just very cute, that's all."

"What are you talking about?

She pinched my cheek, and I writhed with annoyance. "Your whole attitude: smoking, sulking, the whole thing— like you're James Dean or something. It's adorable."

"Shut up."

She lowered her voice like an octave to sound like me. "'Shut up.' So cute."

"Whatever."

"You know what you need?" she said, getting up from the couch, and starting to walk away. "A major tickling!"

She spun around and dove at me, grabbing for my stomach and knees and neck. I started flailing wildly—I'm insanely ticklish—until I was on the floor in front of the TV and Suzanne was sitting on my thighs.

I could barely speak through my hysterics. "Stop!" It wasn't nearly as fun as it used to be.

"That's for calling me Suzie," she said, through her own laughter.

"Okay, okay! I'm sorry—I'll never do it again!"

"You swear?" she said, and poked at my waist one more time. Then she held down my hands over my head so I couldn't defend myself at all.

I nodded, out of breath. "I swear."

"Okay then." She smirked down on me, her face only a few inches from mine. "Cutie," and she gave me a kiss on the cheek before finally getting off me. I lay there, panting. My lungs had taken a serious beating that day. A moment later the phone rang. I knew it would be Lily. Suzanne handed me the cordless.

"Hello?" I was still totally out of breath.

"Simon? Were you just running or something?"

"No. Suzanne was tickling me." I sat up and coughed once. "What's up?"

"I don't know. Nothing."

We went on talking about nothing for about fifteen minutes. She ended by telling me she loved me. I hadn't told her I loved her, and I wasn't about to do it over the phone, so I just said, "I know" and "good-bye," and we hung up.

"Does she smoke?" Suzanne said the moment I'd put down the phone.

"Who?" Like I didn't know.

"Your girlfriend," she said, flipping around with the remote. "I don't even know her name."

"It's Lily."

"Okay. So, does she?"

I shrugged. "Yeah. A little."

"Do you think she'll stop, now that you're going to stop?" She gave me a beat then glared at me. "You are going to stop, right Simon?"

Shrugged again. "Yeah, I am, I am. And I don't know. Probably she would."

"She better, because if you start again because of her, I'll kick her little butt."

I rolled my eyes at her and got up to head upstairs.

"Where you going? I thought we were watching TV here."

"I have to do some reading, and I haven't done any writing in a while."

"Okay. I'm going to come up and bug you later."

When I got to my room, I didn't pick up any book or my journal. I just put on some music, lay on my back on the bed and stared at the cracking paint and plastic stars on the ceiling. After a half hour of thinking about track and Melanie, and cigarettes and Lily, I sat up and looked out the rear window. With the trees bare, I could make out the light traffic on the expressway. I grabbed my journal and started writing. It was just more poetic babbling, I decided, so I flipped to the next blank page and tried to write something with sense. I decided a good place to start would be the story of Aunt Jo coming to get me at school that day. Before I'd gotten to the drive over to the hospital, there was a little rap on the door and Suzanne popped her head in.

"Hello? You're not beating off in here, are you?"

"Fuck you."

She came in and sat down next to me on the bed. "Writing?"

"Mm-hm."

"What about?" She tried to peek at the page.

"Nothing."

"Can I read it?"

"It's not very good."

"Oh, I'm sure it's horrible," she jabbed. "Can I read it anyway?"

I gave it a quick scan, making sure there was nothing too personal. "I guess so. My handwriting's awful, though."

"Same as mine," she said, taking the book from me. She started flipping way back to the front of the journal.

"Hey, come on." I reached for the book and flipped a few pages forward. "It starts here. Don't read that other stuff, okay?"

"Sorry, sorry." She pulled her legs up under her and sort of sat on her heels, then started reading. I couldn't keep my eyes off her while she did, and even though she occasionally tsk'ed—probably at the part about the three of us getting high that morning—I sort of loved watching her read it. I loved watching her eyes go back and forth along each line, and I loved watching her as she slowly turned the page, still reading the last line of the one she was finishing. I loved that she smiled at certain places, and I loved that she frowned and started getting a little teary at others.

"It's not done yet," I said when she reached the end.

She looked at me, frowning but smiling, with tears on each cheek. "Simon," she squeaked, and she threw her arms around me and pressed her cheek up against mine. I tasted salty water. "It's really good."

I was crying a little by the time she pulled away and wiped her eyes. A drop fell onto the open journal, and some ink ran down the page. "Oh, shit," she said, and tried to blot the wet spot. "I'm sorry."

"It's okay, it's okay," I insisted, but she was really upset and reached past me to grab a tissue. "Don't worry about it, Suzie." She patted at the page frantically until I pulled the book away from her, closed it, and set it down on my desk. I don't think I'd ever really had to comfort her before. I thought how odd it was as I rubbed her back.

"You're really good, Simon," she said, now smiling a bit more earnestly. "I had no idea you were that good. I'll let you finish it now." She got up and faced me, her cheeks still wet, and reached out to dry mine with the back of her hand. "I love you, Simon."

I smiled up at her. "Ditto."

She laughed a little and left the room, closing the door behind her. I glanced at the journal on the desk, lay on my back, and hugged my pillow. Eventually, I fell asleep in my clothes with the lights on.

| chapter 14 |

That Saturday night, I stayed at Lily's again. Her mother was due back the next morning, and I got shuffled out the door pretty early to start walking home. I was exhausted when I got there, and it couldn't have been later than eight in the morning, but my mom and dad were both up.

"Why are you home so early?" my mom asked, smiling and hugging me good morning.

"Oh, I couldn't sleep over there, that's all." I'd told them I'd be staying at Noah's. The funny thing is, if they'd known Noah at all, I'm sure they would've rather I'd stayed with Lily. "I think I'll go up to bed, actually," I added, heading upstairs, but a moment later the phone rang.

"Who could this be?" my mom said, grabbing the phone.

"Gee, I don't know," I said with a smile. "Jo, maybe?"

Dad chuckled, but my mom handed the phone to me.

"It's for me?" I took the cordless and put it to my ear, expecting to hear Lily.

"Hi, Simon." Those eyes jumped into my head, greenish, and I saw her hair fall from behind her ear and against her cheek.

"Melanie?" I sat on the top of the stairs, away from prying ears.

"Yup. I didn't wake you, did I?"

"No, but—what are you doing up this early on a Sunday?"

"I get up this early every Sunday," she said, and her voice sang. I could see her smile through the phone. "I was hoping you'd join me for a little run." I pictured her in shorts and a T-shirt, the phone cradled between her shoulder and ear, one foot up on the coffee table, leaning over to tie her running shoes. Of course, she wouldn't be wearing shorts, since it was the dead of winter; it was just a much nicer image than sweats.

"Now?" I said with disbelief.

"Sure."

I was exhausted. I could have fallen asleep that second, I think, right there on the steps. "Um, okay. Yeah."

"Great. Meet me at the track in fifteen."

"Yeah, okay. Bye." She'd already hung up. She was probably already stretching and getting ready to jog over to the school.

I walked into the kitchen. Dad was reading the paper and having herbal tea, his coffee replacement since the stomach pains started. Smells better than it tastes, believe me.

"Thought you were going to bed."

"Yeah, I was." I grabbed the OJ and poured a glass. "Looks like I'm going running instead."

"Hey!" He put down the paper about halfway. "That's great. One of your teammates on the phone?"

"Yeah. I'd better go change." I finally made it to my room and found my sweats. After pulling them on, along with my Yankee hat and running shoes, I headed downstairs and out the door with a "see ya."

It had been a very long time since I'd taken one of these long runs. When I was on the junior high team, even though I was short-distance, I'd run in a few long races. I even joined the cross-country team for a little while. The races were excellent—we'd run through woods and along lakes or streams and huge parks. It was very cool. It was the practices I couldn't stand. All we'd do was run through the neighborhoods in the Hills, the coach nowhere to be seen. Totally useless, and really, really boring. It was those runs that allowed me and Lily to sit behind the school and eventually quit the team.

Melanie was sitting on the grass in the infield doing butterfly stretches when I got there. I could see her breath when she lifted her upper body and called over to me. "Hey, Simon!"

I waved and headed towards her. She'd obviously not bothered showering. Her short hair was back in a tiny ponytail and her face was completely bare—no makeup at all. Made her look sort of paler and younger. It also revealed a few freckles on her nose. A lot of people have that band of freckles over there. I guess that's all I'll have pretty soon. Suzanne's are already practically like that.

I sat down a few feet from her and did some very quick stretching: a few minutes of hurdle stretches, a few of butterfly, and then a quick round of the standing stretches. "So, what course did you want to run?" I asked after we'd both gotten to our feet. She reached down and grabbed her toes. Amazing.

"Oh, I don't know. I was thinking of just sticking to the track."

Of course. How stupid of me. "Okay."

She went on. "Let's just start with a mile or so, and then we could work on some sprints, too."

"Yeah, all right." Anything's better than a long course through the Hills.

We took off into a slow jog around the track. There was no one else around. I wondered if she'd want to talk while we ran.

She did. "Isn't it gorgeous out?" That smile.

"It's pretty cold." Seemed like a sensible reply.

"Ah, we'll warm up in no time." She flipped her head to give me a quick glance. "Wanna pick it up a little?"

"Groan. Yeah, we could try." I smirked at her.

"Come on, smokey," she laughed, and she grabbed my hand as she took off a little faster. She let go a moment later, but I thought I'd throw up. Instead, I coughed. "You'll be all right," she called back, a few paces ahead.

I was all right. My lungs got this dull burn for a little while, but I recognized it was the cold-air burn and tried to breathe through my nose. After a mile of accidentally bumping hands with Melanie about ten times, I think I could have run a marathon.

We spent the rest of the day switching between 200- and 400-yard runs and ended with another mile. This time, Melanie got me started too fast, like a rabbit ought to, and I turned onto the infield after my weak kick and collapsed on the lawn. Melanie was at my side in an instant, smiling down at me.

"Nice job, Simon." She offered me her hand to help me up. I couldn't manage it, so I just shook my head and concentrated on breathing. She sat down next to me and patted my chest. The pain wasn't bad, but I really had like no wind.

Eventually I attempted to speak. "I'm pretty out of shape, huh?" Gasp.

"Nah. You're fine. You're as good a runner as you were in eighth grade."

I sat up, wondering if that was a subtle jab. "I'm exhausted."

"I bet." She glanced at her watch. "I don't have to be home for hours still."

"Well, wanna go down to Sev's and get something to drink?"

"Sure. It's right on the way to my house." Melanie lived in the Hills, closer to the back of the school than the strip mall, by Lily.

It got very cold, walking down to the 7-Eleven still sweaty. Melanie pulled the hood of her sweatshirt on, tucked her hands inside her sleeves, and walked with her arms crossed. God, she looked so cute. I nearly put my arm around to warm her up, but I pussied out.

When we got there, Melanie grabbed a big bottle of vitamin water, and I got a can of iced coffee. "Simon." She gave me a disapproving look.

"What?"

"Are you really gonna drink that? It's horrible for you."

"It's really good."

"Don't you want some water?" She raised her eyebrows and waved her bottle of water before my face like a hypnotist.

"Come on, Melanie. One vice at a time, okay?"

She let up the "naughty" look and dropped her eyebrows. "All right, all right. That sounds fair."

"So, I guess I'll see you tomorrow?" I said as we got out to the parking lot. The 7-Eleven is halfway to Melanie's house from the track. I assumed she'd be heading home straight from there.

"Oh, um, right." She turned and sort of took a step or two backwards away from me as we left the store. "I mean, unless you want to come over for a little while."

She actually seemed nervous. I certainly never thought I'd make Melanie nervous at all. "I think I should probably get home and shower, you know?"

She laughed and pulled the band from her hair. "Right. Okay."

"Seriously, I'd like to, but—"

"It's no problem," she said, waving me off a little. She didn't look nervous anymore. "I'll see you in Rohan's class."

I stood in the 7-Eleven parking lot, watching her walk off. I wanted to run after her, tell her, "Who needs to shower?" and throw my arm around her shoulder, dip her into a ridiculous kiss or something, but I didn't. I just opened my coffee and took a sip and shuddered, then started walking home. There was a message from Lily when I got there, so I called her.

"Hi, Lil."

"Hi, Simon." Here we go—another phone call about nothing.

"What's up? Is your mom home yet?"

"Yeah, she got back a couple of hours ago."

I fiddled with the drawstring on my sweats then started pulling off my sneakers.

"You went running?"

"What?"

"Your mother said you went running when I called."

Sniff. "Yeah. I went up to the track. I was only home for like five minutes this morning."

"By yourself?"

Jesus Christ. I really don't need this. "No, with a few kids from the team."

Lily didn't say a word for at least a minute. I decided not to wait for questions about which kids, and if Melanie was there, and crap like that. "Look, I have to take a shower now. I'm still all sweaty."

"Okay. Will you call me later?"

"Sure. Bye."

"Bye, Simon."

I did call her that night, and she didn't ask about Melanie. She didn't bring up much of anything, really. I don't want it to seem like I didn't like Lily anymore or anything, because I did. I mean, she was still my best friend, I guess, and I was starting to think she was actually very cute most of the time. She was sitting in front of the school the next morning, reading a book. Noah hadn't shown up for the walk, so I was by myself when I reached her.

"Hi, Lil," I said, sitting down on the curb next to her. We had a few minutes before first period. I took her hand.

She smiled at me and kissed me. "Hi. I'm sorry I was so annoying yesterday."

"You weren't. It's okay." She kissed me again. A moment later I noticed Melanie walking toward us and struggled not to look up as she went by.

"Listen," I went on. "I wanted to tell you. My dad is doing really well."

"Oh, that's great!" She beamed at me.

"Yeah. I think he'll probably have surgery soon, and then it'll all be over."

"Oh, Simon, that's so great." She gave me a very melo-dramatic hug.

"Yeah. So, I just wanted to tell you that." I glanced at my green bag. "We should go to class. I can't be late for Rohan anymore."

"I know. Okay." We got up and went inside. Lily gave me a quick hug in the main hall, then headed off to her class. I cut through, past the gym, and went to Rohan's class. Melanie was already there, and I took the desk next to her.

"Hi."

"Hi, Simon." I wondered if she'd noticed Lily and me in front of the school. She didn't hint one way or the other. "Feeling sore today?"

"Yeah, a little bit. It's not so bad, though."

"Good."

Rohan called us to attention and started taking atten-dance. Melanie leaned over a little and whispered to me. "Listen, I didn't mean to get all weird yesterday."

"What do you mean?"

"After we ran, I was being weird. Forget about it, okay?"

I nodded at her—must have looked like a total idiot. But Rohan was calling my name, so I shot him a "here" and Melanie went back to going through her notes. I spent the whole class trying to think of what I could say to her after the period was over. I didn't come up with anything.

"I'll see you at practice, Simon."

"Okay. And don't worry about yesterday. I had a great time." That wasn't bad.

"Good. So did I." And she left.

Practice couldn't come soon enough. I got through my meeting with Rohan pretty easily. Gave him that piece Suzanne had loved so much, and he liked it too. He practically begged me to submit to the journal. I promised to think about it, then took off at four on the dot.

My sweats smelled far less moldy and a bit like Bounce. I changed quickly and sprinted to the track to join Melanie and the others on the far curve for sprints and 400s.

Scott sucked his tongue. "Thanks for joining us, Fisher." Obviously no one had told Scott about my schedule issues.

"I'm going to be late every Monday and Thursday. Didn't Freeman tell you?"

"No, he didn't."

Melanie shrugged at me.

"Get stretched out and take a warm-up in the infield," Captain Scott went on.

"You got it," I quipped as I shot him a thumbs-up and snotty smile, and started jogging along the inside of the fence on the grass. I watched Melanie do a few sprints and a 400 as I jogged. After two laps I returned to Scott and his blocks. Melanie had already worked up a sweat. It seemed like she could barely look at me.

Practice seemed to go on forever. I'd been looking forward to it so I could talk to Melanie, but it's hard to talk when you can hardly breathe and Scott's giving you shit. Scott finally gave the "warm down" command, and I put myself at Melanie's side for a slow lap.

"So, Melanie," I said as we jogged. "I was wondering if you'd want to make a Sunday morning run like a regular thing."

"I always come to the track on Sunday morning, actually." Obviously. God, I'm a moron. "So I guess the question is: do you want to make *joining* me a regular thing?" She looked at me sideways and smiled—cunning. I got the feeling she was much smarter than me . . . or at the very least much more experienced.

"Right," I said as we reached the gym.

Melanie headed toward the girls' locker room. "See you tomorrow."

I got changed and headed home, expecting to find Lily in front of the school. I wasn't disappointed. She took my hand and chewed my ear off as we crossed 25A and through the strip mall. As Lily was saying she wanted to pop into the Gap I heard my name from behind us. I think Lily recognized the voice before I did, because she immediately spun around and got a very tight grip on my arm.

"Hey, wait a sec!" I turned around slowly and saw Melanie on the other side of 25A waving frantically. She was watching the traffic, trying to get across, and occasionally eyeing Lily and me. Her looks meant for us to wait for her. Lily put on some good strength for it, I'll give her that, and we stood there by the curb as Melanie jogged over, her right arm holding her shoulder bag in place and her left hand away from her body and stiff. She looked like anything but a runner just then.

"Hey," she gasped at us. "Hi, Lily."

Lily gave her an ultra-perky hi and hugged my arm tight.

"Listen, Simon," said Melanie, taking on a sort of serious face—tightened up brow and no more smile. "The Frostbite, in Manhattan..." The Frostbite is this ten-mile run in Central Park the New York Road Runners Club has every winter. It's a bitch... I mean, for short-distance smokers, that is. "Registration has to be in by the end of the day tomorrow. If you're interested"—she glanced at Lily—"call me. Okay?"

I felt Lily look up at me. "I don't know, Melanie. Not sure I'm ready for that yet. But I'll think about it."

"That's all I ask," and she shot Lily a friendly sort of *What are we gonna do with him?* smile. "I'll see you guys." She went past us and into the Gap.

Lily didn't feel much like shopping anymore.

FEBRUARY 19

I have a splinter in my foot.
I could poke it
Hold a needle over a candle
Under boiling water
Then pick it out
But I know it would hurt.
So I'll keep walking on it
And no one will notice my limp.

| chapter 15 |

I didn't call Melanie about the Frostbite right away. Truth is, a short-distance runner who still sneaks a cigarette every so often isn't cut out for a ten-mile run in the bitter cold. Besides, I'm no idiot, and neither is Lily. I knew what it would mean if I'd called Melanie and said I wanted to do this major run with her all day in the city. And I wasn't really amped about the repercussions.

So it was a couple of days later I guess, I was cutting across from the gym over to the science wing when I bumped into Noah and Goody, his new best friend.

"Simon." Noah stopped me and nodded at Goody, who smirked and walked on. "I gotta talk to you, dude."

"You're hanging with that asshole a lot, dude," I said. Dude, dude, dude.

Noah got pissed real quick. "He's an asshole?" he practically shouted. "You're the fucking asshole, Fisher." Suddenly he was pushing me, like shoving my shoulders with both hands real hard, acting like a real jock asshole.

"You think I don't notice your fucking behavior lately, Fisher?" He kept ranting at me. I didn't even know how to react. "You think no one can tell you're all over Melanie's jock, while Lily just stands there like your little lapdog?"

"What?" I might have feigned a little incredulousness. "Dude, that's ridiculous." I started to walk away, but Noah grabbed my shoulder.

"You know what your problem is, don't you, Fisher, you pervert?"

That stopped me. Fine, maybe I was crushing on Siegel a little. But come on, she was hot—doesn't make me a pervert.

"I know why you're into Melanie, man." He smirked at me. Made me wanna retch. "Cute little thing, freckles, barely a nose on her face. Remind you of anyone?"

"Who?" My face started getting a little warm. My brain wasn't totally going there yet; I could see it from down the road, though. And I didn't like it.

"Suzanne, you pervert. You're so hot for your sis—"

I punched him. Hard. And he went down in a flash. His nose was bloody, but he was laughing.

"Whatever, Fisher," he said through his hand as he started to get up. "Fucking perv."

"Fuck you, Noah." And I walked off.

When I got home after school that day, Suzanne was sleeping, and Mom and Dad were hanging around in the living room. Dad turned off the music when I came in, but I only said hi quick and picked up the phone.

I got her voice mail. "Hi, Melanie. It's Simon. I know it's too late for me to register, but I was thinking about going with you to the Frostbite. Um . . . call me back."

In my head, it was already done. I was already there—past smoking, and past Lily and that whole depressing situation, and if I never saw Noah again, it would be too soon. I decided, probably right when Noah hit the ground, that I had my own little cancer to fight, and it was growing fast in me, and the best way to beat it was to run.

Dad was beating his cancer. Surgery was scheduled for a month from then, the Monday after the Frostbite. And since they'd stopped the chemo—I guess since it had already done all it could do without causing him more harm than good—Dad had been feeling a lot better. He even went into work a couple of times that week. And Suzanne went back up to Boston.

I started training more seriously with Melanie pretty much right away. After I'd left her that voice mail, she'd immediately called me back, pretty excited, and told me that there was late registration for an extra twenty bucks, which of course my folks were completely dying to give me, along with the rest of the entrance fee. Melanie was fucking giddy. Lily wasn't.

If I'd had any balls whatsoever, I would have just broken up with her, told her I didn't want her for my girlfriend anymore—that I never really did. That if I wanted to cure myself of my crap I had to quit smoking, start running again, do everything to make my dad feel better about me. But I didn't have any balls.

Lily was sulking on the curb after I'd told her I was going to run the Frostbite after all. "But, Simon," she said, glaring up at me through a squint, "you don't even like long-distance races."

I paced around in front of her and fingered the lighter in my pocket, dying to light up. "That's not the point. . . ."

"Yes it is. That's completely the point." She got to her feet. She was getting angry, which is something Lily doesn't really get very often. "Because the real reason you're doing this stupid run is so you can drool all over Melanie Siegel." Before I could say anything, she flew on. "It's totally obvious. You're completely in love with her!"

So I just turned and walked off. Which I know is completely shitty of me. But what could I have done? Stayed and lied to her, told her that she was wrong and that I loved her, not Melanie? Told her that I didn't want anything to happen with Melanie, and I was really happy being with her? Or would it have been better to tell her the truth, that I didn't feel anything for her, and that making out with her was pretty boring, while Melanie accidentally brushing my hand during warm-ups was about the hottest thing ever? No, really neither option seemed so great to me. So I just went to class, English, and sat down next to Melanie.

The next week was complete hell. I worked my sorry ass off at practice every day, well enough even to feed Scott back his stupid little smirks. I beat him in the 400-yard run twice in one afternoon that Friday, and Melanie was there at the finish line in high-five pose.

"Nice, Simon!" she practically screamed as I tried not to smile and slapped her hand. For a minute it reminded me of Noah and his idiotic high fives, but I shook that off and walked to the infield with Melanie to jog inside the fence for a warm-down. Scott shuffled up beside us on the track side of the fence.

"Nice job, Fisher," he said. "I guess Siegel's had a good effect on you." He winked at her. I almost threw up. He finally jogged ahead and Melanie laughed.

"You like that guy?" I looked at the frozen grass under my feet as it crunched with each step.

"Scott?" Melanie exhaled. "I guess he's kind of a tool, but whatever."

"Yeah he is," I replied, and I chuckled. Melanie chuckled back.

"Jealous?"

I looked up at her and caught her smirking at me sideways. She was dancing this fine line between flirting and making fun of me. "What? Why would I be jealous of that tool?"

She just laughed, and as we finished our lap and the practice started to fall apart, she grabbed my hand and we ran toward the gym.

We probably looked pretty stupid, like a pair of completely corny idiots, laughing as we ran top speed down the gentle slope across the lawn from the track to the locker rooms. And when I saw Lily walking along the south path with Noah, I didn't even care. It was easier this way. Let her think what she wants, I thought, and let Noah kiss my ass. They could go screw each other's brains out, stoned to the tits, for all I cared. And they probably would, too.

| chapter 16 |

By the time the Frostbite came around, I was really beginning to feel like my old self again on the track. Melanie and I had spent hours, outside of regular track practice, training for it. We even ran the course through the Hills a few times and I barely minded. At that point, it had been nearly a month since my last cigarette, and aside from the odd brown goop I'd cough up in the shower some mornings, I wasn't feeling it at all.

Just before I left the house the morning of the run, the phone rang. Five thirty in the goddamn morning. I snapped it up in the middle of the first ring so the whole house wouldn't wake up. I half expected it to be Aunt Jo. But really even she doesn't call that early. Instead it was Lily. For once she didn't want to talk about nothing.

"I just wanted to wish you good luck," she said.

"With what?" I asked. "Do you know it's five thirty in the goddamn morning?"

Lily was silent. She might have been crying.

"With your run," she finally said. "And with everything. . . . Your dad."

I took a deep breath and let it out, loud. "He's fine. He's going to be completely fine by Tuesday morning, okay?"

"Okay," Lily said back, kind of in a whisper.

She was pathetic and it was pissing me off. So I just said what I had to say. "Listen, Lily. You probably shouldn't call here anymore. I mean, I'm not smoking anymore, or drinking or getting high or anything."

I paused for a minute to decide if I should go on. It was long enough for Lily to stammer, "And you're with Melanie Siegel now, too, right?"

"Fine, right," I snapped back. Why did she have to make this so hard? "I just . . . I don't want those things in my life anymore."

"What things?" Lily asked. She spat the words out. "Me? Me and Noah?"

"Yes." Now I was whispering. "I just want to be normal. Melanie is . . . normal."

And Lily hung up. I started walking to the Long Island Rail Road station.

I met Melanie at the LIRR at six and we boarded the train to Penn Station. As soon as I saw her on the platform, I felt pretty good about everything I had said to Lily. She wasn't smoking, or sulking on a curb, or wearing baggy black clothes. She was just standing, looking at her watch, holding a bottle of some weird vegetable juice or something, and bouncing a little to keep warm. I closed my eyes a minute, got Lily out of my head, and went over to her—smiling.

The ride into midtown Manhattan is about forty-five minutes. That meant the longest time I'd spent with Melanie while not running. I sipped my station coffee as we rumbled along. It was not good coffee, but it was full of sugar and cream and held my attention since I couldn't think of a single thing to say. Melanie sipped her weird juice and looked out the window. For a moment I watched her; she seemed nervous again as she sat across from me in one of those five-seaters. Suddenly she looked up and caught me staring.

Now there was eye contact, so I smiled a little. "Um, you think I'll be able to finish?" I said. She looked away quickly. "The race, I mean."

She shrugged in reply and took another sip. "I think so." She didn't look back at me, but kept her eyes out the window as we pulled into the Jamaica station and the doors opened. I watched a man in paint-splattered pants and a pea coat get on the train and the doors closed. "We've been training pretty hard."

"I guess," I said. "But the most I've ever run in one go is a 10K I did two years ago, and that's barely six miles."

Melanie looked at me, right in the eyes, for several moments.

"What?" I pulled my coffee away from my face and turned to her.

She got up from her bench and dropped down next to me, took my hand. "Have you broken up with Lily?"

"What?" I said. Where the hell did that come from? "I don't know. I think so." What the hell was I saying? "I mean . . ."

"You mean . . . ?" She leaned away from me and raised her eyebrows at me. *Loser.*

"I mean, I talked to her this morning, and we're done." There.

"Good," she said, and she slid her hand into mine. I turned to look at her, first at her hand, then at her face. She was smiling, and her crooked little smile made my stomach flip. "Kiss me, then."

"Oh." I leaned closer to her slowly and went to touch her cheek. "I have coffee breath. . . ."

But she just rolled her eyes and planted her mouth on mine. It knocked the wind out of me; I felt air rushing out of every pore in my body. Our hands parted and I held on to her waist and kissed her harder. Eventually we pulled apart and I exhaled slowly. Her eyes were closed for a moment, but then she opened them and smiled.

"Now that wasn't so hard, was it?" she quipped. Then she sidled up closer to me and leaned on my arm, sipping her disgusting juice. I looked down at her for a moment, then turned back to the window and my coffee, and smiled.

We pulled into Penn Station before seven, and walked across town to the 6 train to make it up to the start for sign-in and tag pick-up. Melanie switched between holding my arm and my hand as we walked along Thirty-third Street.

"Simon?" she said as we started down the steps to the station at Park Avenue. "What's going on with you?"

No, not now. We're not doing this now. "What do you mean?" As if I didn't know.

"I don't know—you've been so . . . you seemed like you were going to lose it, I guess." She stepped up the nearest MetroCard vending machine and held out her hand. I gave her a five and said it was on me. She rolled her eyes again. "You know what I mean, Simon." She handed me a one-trip and we turned to the turnstiles. "I mean, everyone knows you liked to get high and all that, which, whatever, really. I don't care."

"Is that all you mean?" I kicked around at nothing on the platform and glanced up the track looking for headlights.

"No, no," she said, staring at the cement under her feet. "I mean . . . I know you've been upset about something lately, and I didn't want to push you to talk about it or anything, but I just—"

"It's nothing, Melanie." I had to stop her. I couldn't watch her squirm with it anymore, especially knowing that if I dropped the *C* word on her, she'd absolutely crumble under the weight of it. "I mean, it's all okay now. I'm not upset anymore."

"Prom?"

I looked up at her. What? And where was this fucking train?

"Promise?"

Ah. God, she was fucking cute and precious. "Yes, I promise. It's fine." Headlights. Thank god.

| chapter 17 |

"You're going to wait for me at the start, right?" I said to Melanie as we separated to get our bibs, me from *A* through *F*, and her from *R* through *Z*. "I'm not running this hell alone, you know."

"Of course," she said as she jogged off. "I'll be right over there"—she pointed to a crowded table a little way off from the start line—"by the Road Runners table."

I watched her run off for a moment, then headed to the table.

"Fisher." The woman behind the table smiled at me and then looked down at her list.

"Simon?"

"That's me," I replied with a smile I hoped wasn't too obviously sarcastic.

"Okay," she said, handing me a bib with 2157 on it and a blank line along the bottom. "Hey, it looks like you're one of only twenty runners under sixteen today, Simon. Way to go!"

Wow, I am? "Um, thanks."

"Okay. Well, you need to fill out that line at the bottom with your emergency contact information, a name and a phone number of who we should call if you have a medical emergency—"

"Can I just put 911?" I smiled at her.

"Oh, no, dear," she said as if I'd genuinely misunderstood. "Put your parents' names or someone we should call in an emergency."

Yikes. "Okay. And then I'm all set?"

"That's right. Oh, do you have someone who can pin that to your back for you?"

I glanced over at Melanie. She was leaning over *R* through *Z*, laughing easily and writing furiously on that emergency-contact black line. "Yeah, I do." I grabbed a pen and scribbled down "David Fisher" and our home phone number, then picked up a few safety pins from the table and headed over to the Road Runners table to wait for Melanie.

Pretty soon she bounded up to me and grabbed my bib. "Turn around," she ordered, so I did. Then she handed me her bib—number 103; jeez, she must have registered about fifteen seconds after they started taking names—and turned her back to me, pulling her hair up to expose the back of her sweatshirt.

I struggled to get the pin through the bib and her sweats, and I'm pretty sure I pricked her at least once, but I finally got it done. Before she turned back around to face me, I put my hands on her shoulders and rubbed them a little. Now that I had a girlfriend I wanted to put my hands on, I didn't really have any idea how. But she leaned her head back and gave me an "Mmmm" in return.

"Are you ready?" she said as she started stretching a little.

"I think so." I gave a little effort to reaching my toes, which I could really never do, then gave up and did a few hurdles and just kind of shuffled in place to loosen up.

The other runners were gathering right up at the start line, and since Melanie and I are in the youngest age group, and since I had exactly zero RR runs under my belt at this point, we agreed to start in the back. It was quite a few awkward minutes, even after the gun went off, before we could move back there, so we just shuffled around and checked out the other runners. That woman at the table was right; I didn't see anyone else who looked to be in high school. I told Melanie about it.

"Well," she said as we started picking up a little speed, "that's because we're made of awesome." I laughed. "How about one for the road?" she said, and she leaned in and kissed me again. "Let's go."

The five-mile mark: I'm breathing through a haze, and the cold air makes the top of my nostrils burn. I can hear my feet hitting the path through Central Park. But I can't feel them.

I drop my head and look at her feet. "Melanie," I say, getting up to her stride, always dangerous, "it was my dad."

Her left hand grazes my right. She doesn't look at me. I'm not sure she heard me, really.

"It was cancer," I say between breaths. "But it's going to be fine." Breathe. Breathe. "After Monday, it's going to be fine."

I did finish. Melanie stuck with me through the whole thing, although I'm fairly sure it killed her every time some fucking octogenarian passed us. I might be exaggerating, but really, not by much. I think Melanie could have finished in under ninety minutes, which would have been great, but thanks to me, we barely broke the top five in the seventy-plus group.

My time didn't matter, though. By the time I got home, showered, and passed out in my bedroom, I had cured myself. I finished ten miles, I sweated out all that nicotine, and I felt like all the hate had left with it, like a fucking toxin. I was light-headed and giddy, probably dehydrated. I thought about Melanie and smiled and got hard, but I was too tired to even commit to a few pumps. So I rolled over and stared at the bright red numbers next to the bed. As the clock blinked over to 2:30, I fell asleep. And early in my dreams I heard the front door open downstairs as Suzanne got home. The countdown to surgery had begun. But I was safe, and clean. And Dad would be safe soon, because I'd beaten everything—smoking, getting high, Lily and Noah—and finally I was normal.

Of course, I was kidding myself. Splinters go much deeper than that.

| chapter 18 |

You want to know something about surgery? There's not just surgeons, like you might think. Nope, not in Manhattan. In Manhattan there's probably one famous joker in a ridiculous outfit for every single minute part of your fucking body. Need surgery on your right ass cheek? We'll form a team! We have an ass specialist, and this right-cheek specialist, and this one here in the green leisure suit and red sneakers is a fucking whiz at assholes. A left-cheek specialist will be in the OR—you know, scrubbed and on the clock!—but will only get involved if they need him.

For my dad they had the one dude we'd been with all along. He was the cancer king—Abe's fucking genius. He'd go in to cut the fucker out of my dad and throw it into the Hudson I guess. But here's the thing: the cancer was all tangled up. Yeah, it was tiny now, and all that. But

272

it was tangled up among veins and capillaries and arteries and various other important shit a person can't just slice away at. Not without making my dad bleed like a fucking cow undergoing strict kosher slaughter. So that's where the vascular surgeon comes in. He greeted us in the waiting room when we arrived: me, my mom, Suzanne, Jo, and Uncle Abe. Mom and I and Suzanne had already watched Dad get rolled off after his pre-op interview, which isn't as fun as it sounds.

"Smoke?" the intern had asked.

"Quit," Dad said. He glanced at me.

"Me too," I threw in.

"When did you quit?" the intern asked.

"A month ago," I said. But he wasn't talking to me.

"Four years ago," my dad replied. He glanced at me again.

I squinted at him: four years ago? How did I not know that? I'd always assumed he quit with my mom, before I existed.

But the intern went on: what drugs have you taken? when did you eat last? drink? alcohol?

Finally he left, and I told my dad I'd buy him a steak after this was over.

"And a beer!" he said. And I love you.

I love you too.

The vascular surgeon thrust his hand at my uncle, who took it and smiled with half his face.

"I'm Dr. V____." Something. I'm not trying to be coy or protect the innocent or anything. I just can't remember his name. But I can remember his face, and his hairline, and his clothes. He looked like a clown on the make or something. I'm not even kidding: bright blue double-breasted suit that was probably GQ in about 1987 and this tie that looked like Jackson Pollock attacked it with McDonald's condiment packets. And French cuffs. Somebody line up everyone who wears French cuffs so I can tell them all to fuck off at once.

Meanwhile, from about day one, there was the idea that hey, worst comes to worst, let's just get rid of that pesky old pancreas. So the pancreatic specialist is all hanging out, ready to get to work. I didn't meet that guy. Who knows if he ever made it to the OR. As it turns out, they never needed him anyway.

Suzanne and I were sitting in the speckled gray chairs. Her arm was around my shoulders as we watched the adults converge at the center of the OR waiting room.

"Looks just like my dorm lounge," Suzanne said, glancing around the room.

I watched my uncle move closer to Dr. V. Abe bends a little at the waist and shoulders when he talks to about anyone. He sticks his neck out and lowers his head, just so he can hear whatever short person is talking to him. He pulls his glasses to one of three places: his forehead, the tip of his nose, or all the way off his face. He nods a lot, and asks questions I don't always understand in a slow, deliberate voice with a New York accent few living people still use. How many *t*'s in "bottle"? Wrong. The answer is none. That's the accent.

Dr. V cowered a little. That's usually how people react to Abe's lean-in. Mom moved in a little too, and Jo took her arm and joined her. "We're just waiting right now for the anesthesia to take full effect."

"Mm-hm," Mom said. She looked so tired. Her eyes were red, and her face seemed to be sliding off her skull. Not to sound morose. It was really like her head had no strength left to hold on. Jo rubbed her sister's arm and patted her wrist.

The doctor glanced at Abe, then put his hand on Mom's shoulder. "Mrs. Fisher?" he said. They'd never met.

"Diane," my mom said. I was surprised she didn't admonish his use of "Mrs." She's very outspoken usually about "Ms." versus "Mrs."

"I know you spoke with . . ." That super cancer doctor. I don't remember his name either. "And he told you and David all about the operation, how it will go."

Mom nodded. Suddenly she looked very lost. Her head swiveled, looking for us—for me and Suzanne. Mom looked tiny. Something like an old widow, but more like a lost girl.

"Come on, Simon," Suzanne said. She pulled her arm off my shoulder and briskly rubbed my thigh through my jeans. Then she got up and went to Mom.

I followed and soon Mom had her arm around my shoulders.

Jo smiled weakly, though her eyes were red. She stood behind the Fishers and grasped my shoulder. "These are David's babies," she said. "Suzanne and Simon."

The doctor smiled at us, then looked back at my mom. He was still smiling as he started in again. "This is a delicate operation. It's going to be a long surgery. I'm going to suggest that once I leave you now to go scrub up, you take a walk. Get out of here. If you just sit in the waiting room, you'll drive yourselves crazy."

Mom waved the idea off and turned her head away. "I can't eat."

"Me either," Jo agreed.

I glanced at my uncle. He slid his glasses up to the bridge of his nose. "Come on, Diane." He put his big arm around my mom. She released me and Suzanne and returned the half-hug. "We don't have to eat, but sitting here won't help anything."

The doctor nodded and thanked Abe, like he'd been comforting to my mom as a personal fucking favor to Dr. V. "Come back after supper, and then it's the waiting game. If you don't hear from us again before nine tonight, we're in the clear. So no news is good news."

He looked square at me. "All right, Simon?"

I squinted at him. My eyes burned a little.

What the fuck are you asking me for?

But he was asking me, like I was the official family representative. Hate to break it to you, doc, but you got the wrong man. Did I say "man"?

"Okay," Suzanne said. I felt her hand close over mine. Protection. "Nine, got it." She smiled and pulled me away.

Jo hurried along after us and took my elbow. "Is Italian okay?" she said. "There's a place right downstairs."

The sisters practically carried me to the elevator and down to the main lobby and out to Seventh Avenue. It was raining, so the three of us jogged across Seventh. We stepped into the little restaurant and Jo shook out her coat.

We chose a table toward the back, just me, Jo, and Suzanne, and the waitress handed us our menus. I recognized a man sitting at the next table to ours.

"Who's that?" I whispered to Suzanne. "I know that guy."

Suzanne glanced up and shrugged.

"No, seriously," I insisted, a little louder. "He's some comedian or something. Some old-time comedian."

Jo turned around in her seat to see. She's never shy about approaching celebrities young or old in the city. "Is it Alan King?" she whispered to me.

"I think he's dead," Suzanne said. "I'm getting some wine."

"You're not twenty-one," I said.

"I'm close enough," Suzanne said with an eyebrow cock.

"You're not, Simon," Jo added quickly. "Your mom would kill me in a heartbeat if I let you drink, you know."

"I don't even want one," I said as the waiter came over. "Jeez. Just 'cause Suzie's a lush . . ."

We ordered and sat in silence for a long time. Jo tried to get us talking a bit, but Suzanne wasn't having it. When my gnocchi hit the table, I pushed it around with my fork. Jo stabbed at her salad.

"So, how come nine is, like, the magic number tonight?" I asked.

Suzanne looked up at Jo. "What do you mean?" Suzanne asked.

"Oh come on," I said. I dropped my fork onto the pasta and stared at it. "The doctor said if he doesn't come talk to us before nine, it's good. No news is good news, remember?"

"The surgery is very delicate," Jo said. "That's all he meant. And if there haven't been any problems by that time, Daddy will be pretty much out of the woods."

"Right," Suzanne added. "But don't worry. These are the best doctors in the world, I'm pretty sure."

I listened, and I heard them, but it didn't register. Something had grabbed me when that doctor looked square at me and said "all right." There was something I was supposed to know, some role I was supposed to play. His words were like a lasso around my belly, and they jerked me forward a hundred feet from where I'd been. I didn't know where I'd landed. I still hadn't opened my eyes.

Jo carefully poked a sliver of parmesan cheese onto her fork and then added a piece of romaine. "Of course they are," she said. "That's what Abe does. He knows the best and he gets the best."

"Dad's gonna die," I suddenly blurted out.

Suzanne dropped her fork and her arms shook, like she had a chill.

"That's what he meant, the doctor," I added.

Suzanne threw her arms around me. She shook her head and buried it into the curve of my shoulder and neck.

I nodded. "He is. That's what he meant. That's what he thought I already knew. He looked right at me. 'All right' didn't just mean 'okay.' He was seeing if I'd be all right. He meant 'Are you ready to not have a father around? Or are you a baby?'"

Jo started tearing up. She took my free hand and held it. "He didn't mean that at all, Simon," she said. "Just by saying 'all right'? How could he have meant that?"

But I knew I was right. It was in his eyes. "This is a nearly impossible surgery," the eyes meant. "We're probably not going to pull it off. Take care of your mother and sister if you can."

I said it over and over to myself, in my head: *He's going to die.* But I didn't cry. I expected to bawl and bawl at any second, but I only got angry.

"Why didn't anyone tell me?" I managed to squeak out. "Why didn't anyone say 'Your dad is gonna die'?"

Jo and Suzanne exchanged a fucking glance. Very typical.

I took a big bite of my dinner. "What time is it?" I asked, my mouth full.

Suzanne glanced at her watch. It was this retro eighties looking thing, colorful and cute. Inappropriate. "Almost eight."

"I'm going back now," I said, getting up.

"Simon, wait . . ."

I heard Jo whisper to my sister as I reached the door: "It's okay, go after him. I'll take care of the check."

As I pushed through the door, I heard Suzanne's chair scrape the floor. "Simon."

I hit Seventh Avenue. The rain was getting heavier. From across the street, the red hand stopped me. DON'T WALK.

"Simon, please wait."

"I am waiting," I answered, looking right at the red hand. Suzanne took my hand, and I pulled it away.

"Why didn't you tell me?" I snapped at her.

"Simon," she said. "Simon, you knew how sick Dad was too."

"Everyone said he was getting better," I said back. I was practically shouting. "Everyone said this surgery would be the end of it. That he'd be healthy again."

"No one ever said he'd be healthy again." She tried to hug me, but I pushed her away and looked for the walk signal. It was there, so I bolted across Seventh. Suzanne caught me as I reached the hospital awning.

"You want to know the truth?" she said as she took my wrist. Her voice was thin and strained. "Mom and Dad tried to be honest with you."

I glared at her.

"They sat us down," she went on. My belly flipped. "They tried to talk to you. . . . You wouldn't listen. You refused to listen."

So that was it. I was still a baby—still a little boy tugging at his stupid white socks and staining his face with tears and spit and soil.

Suzanne let go of my wrist. Her shoulders sagged. "I'm sorry, Simon. It's time to grow up."

But I had one more tantrum in me. In anger and frustration I stomped into the hospital and found the elevator, pounded the 7 button and the door close button. With my eyes on my sneakers, I strode through the OR waiting room.

Mom called to me, but didn't get up. I glanced at her. Abe took her arm: *Let him alone.*

Into the men's room. Cold water at full blast. I splashed it over my face and head, then leaned on the mirror and stared at my eyes. They were red and black and purple. Tears mingled with the rain water and tap water. I reached to my right for a paper towel, but the dispenser was empty. I gritted my teeth and locked my jaw. My temples ached. I drew back and punched the empty dispenser. My fist throbbed. I lifted my fist over my head and brought it down on the top of the dispenser like a blacksmith hammer.

BANG.

Again, I raised it up and swung it down.

BANG.

Again.

BANG.

Again.

BANG, BANG, BANG. And my arm kept going until I nearly fell. The dispenser had come clean off the wall. Where it had been was only bent brackets and crumbling plaster. My last tantrum felt pretty much over.

I stood over the busted towel dispenser, breathing heavily and just kind of trying to catch my breath a little. I felt a little better, honestly. I mean, I knew it was pretty stupid and obviously wouldn't make everything right, but for a few minutes, I felt totally relaxed and okay. And then this old janitor walked in.

He was a black guy, like a hundred years old, probably. He was wearing one of those green custodian uniforms, head to toe, and carrying a bucket with a rag and some spray bottles in it.

"Good evening, son," he said to me. I just looked at him. "Are we having a problem with that dispenser again?" He laughed a little and smiled at me, then bent over and picked the thing up and placed it on the counter under the mirror.

"Oh," I mumbled. "No, I'm sorry. I did that."

"Ah, I see," he said. "Make you feel better?" He sprayed his rag and started wiping down the mirror in big circles.

I thought about it again. "Not really. I mean, for a second it did. But not really."

He sprayed his rag again and started another series of circular wipes on the countertop. "No, I don't suppose it would." He tossed his rag back into his bucket and lifted the busted dispenser under his arm. "Some folks who come through here," he said as he turned to head back out of the bathroom, "seem to feel better when they speak to God." Then he smiled and nodded at me. "I'll pray for your father, son." He pushed the door and walked out.

"Thanks." Half of me meant it, too. Seriously, half of me was casting Morgan Freeman in his role in the goddamn story of my life. I mean, the other half was telling him to go fuck off and die.

I walked over to the mirror and stared. My eyes were red; it seemed like it had been months since they weren't. Probably no one even thinks for a second I stopped getting high, the way my eyes must look to them. I turned on the cold tap and splashed my face a few times, then remembered the towels problem, so I just stood there and let my face drip for a few seconds.

"Knock knock." It was Suzanne.

"Yeah," I replied through the door. What is this, Grand Central Station? I thought I was in the most private room in the damn hospital.

"You all right in here, Simon?" she said, peeking in. I turned to her, and I guess my face was dripping so she probably thought I was crying. "Oh, Simon," she said, like it was a major thing to find me crying these days anyway. She rushed in and put her arms around me, her back to the mirror. I pulled her against me, desperate, and looked over her shoulder at us. There was the same hair tangling together, like we were the same head, and I saw my hazel eyes there, so red around the edges, and I saw that I *was* crying. I was fucking bawling, and I felt Suzanne shaking, quivering, just fucking belching with tears.

I turned my head a little to see her face, but I didn't want her to pull back from me, and she turned too. And then our lips met, sort of by accident, but we were kissing, and I tasted her tears, or my tears—our tears running down our freckled cheeks and between our lips. Suzanne's whole body shook with crying spasms, and I pulled her in tighter, savoring the saltiness on her lips. Tighter. Never let go.

"Son." The janitor was outside the door suddenly, and he was knocking. How long had he been knocking?

We pulled apart and just looked at each other, both of us wet and swollen with grief and god knows what else.

"Son, the doctor is out here."

The doctor is back. The doctor is back. This means something. I grabbed Suzanne by the wrist and she shook, like she'd been asleep, and I checked the time. It was eight forty-five.

It was eight forty-five. The doctor was early. "Suzanne."

"Simon," she said, quivering a little. "Simon . . . I'm sorry."

I just looked at her, and she really broke down. Like, dropped to her knees and sobbed. I knew why she was sobbing, but I knew I couldn't get close to her anymore, and I knew I couldn't stay there, so I just flung through the door, right past the janitor, and I saw my mom and Jo and Abe, and the doctor was there, and he was in scrubs and that blue gown, and it had blood on it, and they all looked at me, and my mom called my name, I think.

But I ran past them, right to the stairs, and I took them two at a time and burst through the door into a wet night and I ran. I ran down Seventh Avenue, right in the left lane. I just ran, and the mist covered my face. It was so fine, but after just a block it had drenched me, and I licked my lips once more to find the salt that had been left there by our tears, but it was gone already, washed away, dripping down my front and into the street as I ran.

MARCH 9

Ask me how Dad died.
"Cancer," I'll say.
But cancer never killed him.
Those men gathered around him—
masked like outlaws.

They tried to cut it out. And
That's when he bled.
That's when he died.

SUZANNE

The storm door opened, and closed. And seconds later, opened again, closed again. It reminded me of a holiday, with people arriving constantly—a stream of people, carrying food I could smell from upstairs. But there was no loud joyous hello, no "nu?"—just the door and the food. And the smell of food still climbed upstairs and got past my bedroom door and through my old quilt, and it found me curled up in the corner of my bed. I shivered.

I wasn't crying anymore, just lying silently in a ball, like my old dress and new tights in front of my closet door.

I whispered, "Simon," and hoped he could somehow hear me and would come in and help me. He was fifteen steps away, hiding out in his own room, but I couldn't go to him, not like I used to.

Exhaustion washed over me, and it was a relief. Half of my mind was already escaping to sleep, while the other half heard Mom's voice: "Simon, where's Suzie?"

He wouldn't come get me, I knew. But the delirium was spreading—from one half of my brain to the other—and soon he was holding my hand.

I was holding his; his was limp, and I was like a toddler dragging a ragdoll across the cement. In a mixture of memory and dream, we were standing in a parking lot— wide and bleak—under a darkening early-evening sky. I looked down at my doll, and there was Simon—was he eight? Ten? Thirteen?

Thirteen, I realized, because he was in his suit, and his eyes were swollen from crying, because Grandpa had died.

"Dad died," I muttered, and then it was silent.

I looked up again, and the grass was white, blanketed in a thin coat of new snow, and a soccer goal with no net stood over us. Across the field was a swing set, and both swings soared back and forth, not quite in rhythm. The sun was still low, but it was morning now. I was dropping Simon at school, after a painful, long weekend.

Thirteen-year-old Simon let go of my hand and smiled at me. He forgot so quickly. I wanted to tell him I love him as he ran off, but when I tried to speak, my tongue became swollen. Across the field, one of the swings stopped suddenly and the dark-haired girl hopped off and waved. The other swinger hollered, "Si-MUN!" and I jumped at the broken silence.

I looked down at my butterfly tights, then at the trio at the swings. Simon settled onto one and began to sway. The other boy called out again as he bounced before his friends: "Si-MUN."

The sun was over the treeline to the east, and I heard Simon's laugh, then the girl's. The other boy guffawed sarcastically. They were beautiful, in their way. All of it was beautiful.

But behind them, the rear entrance to the school was opening slowly, and though I tried to shout, I couldn't make a sound.

| acknowledgments |

Thanks to my editor, Andrew Karre, for having enough faith in the seed of this book to see it through, and to the rest of the crew at Carolrhoda and Lerner. Thanks also to Edward Necarsulmer IV; here's hoping I live up to the big things you've got planned. And thanks to all the good teachers—and some of the bad ones too.

A special thanks goes to Adela Peskorz and all the members of Teens Know Best in Saint Paul. I know how lucky I am to have had help from such a talented, intelligent, and creative group of readers.

Thanks of course to my family, particularly my mother and brother on opposite coasts. Also thanks to MIL, FIL, and SILs for the babysitting so I could work. And huge thanks to my wife, Beth, for so much love and support and dozens of first reads, and to my son, Sam, for making every day feel like magic.